The
DAYDREAMER

The
DAYDREAMER

IAN McEWAN

illustrated by

ANTHONY BROWNE

Scholastic Inc.

New York   Toronto   London   Auckland   Sydney

ISBN 0-590-88018-7

Text copyright © 1994 by Ian McEwan.
Illustrations copyright © 1994 by Anthony Browne.
All rights reserved. Published by Scholastic Inc., 555 Broadway,
New York, NY 10012, by arrangement with HarperCollins Children's Books,
a division of HarperCollins Publishers

12 11 10 9 8 7 6 5 4 3 2 1   6 7 8 9/9 0 1/0

Printed in the U.S.A.   40

First Scholastic printing, September 1996

To Polly, Alice, William, and
Gregory—with thanks

My purpose is to tell of bodies which have been transformed into shapes of a different kind.

Ovid, *Metamorphoses*, Book One

The DAYDREAMER

CHAPTER ONE

INTRODUCING PETER

WHEN PETER FORTUNE was ten years old, grown-up people sometimes used to tell him he was a difficult child. He never understood what they meant. He didn't feel difficult at all. He didn't throw bottles at the garden wall, or tip ketchup over his head and pretend it was blood, or slash at his granny's ankle with his sword, though he occasionally thought of these things. Apart from all vegetables except potatoes, and fish, eggs, and cheese, there was nothing he would not eat. He wasn't noisier or dirtier or more stupid than anyone he knew. His name was easy to say and spell. His face, which was pale and freckled, was easy enough to remember. He went to school every day like all other children and never made that much fuss about it. He was only as horrid to his sister as she was to him. Policemen never came knocking at the front door wanting to arrest him. Doctors in white coats never offered to take him away to the madhouse. As far as Peter was concerned, he was really quite easy. What was difficult about him?

It was not until he had been a grownup himself for many years that Peter finally understood. They thought he was difficult because he was so silent. That seemed to bother people. The other problem was he liked being by himself. Not all the time, of course. Not even every day. But most days he liked to go off somewhere for an hour—to his bedroom, or the park. He liked to be alone and think his thoughts.

Now, grown-ups like to think they know what's going on inside a ten-year-old's head. And it's impossible to know what someone is thinking if they keep quiet about it. People would see Peter lying on his back on a summer's afternoon, chewing a piece of grass and staring at the sky. "Peter. Peter! What are you thinking about?" they would call to him. And Peter would sit up with a start. "Oh, nothing. Nothing at all." Grown-ups knew that something was going on inside that head, but they couldn't hear it or see it or feel it. They couldn't tell Peter to stop it, because they did not know what it was he was doing in there.

He could have been setting his school on fire or feeding his sister to an alligator and escaping in a hot-air balloon, but all they saw was a boy staring at the blue sky without blinking, a boy who did not hear you when you called his name.

As for being on his own, well, grown-ups didn't much like that either. They don't even like other grown-ups being on their own. When you join in, people can see what you're up to. You're up to what they're up to. You have to join in, or you'll spoil it for everyone else. Peter had different ideas. Joining in was all very fine in its place. But far too much of it went on. In fact, he thought, if people spent less time joining in and making others join in, and spent a little time each day alone remembering who they were or who they might be, then the world would be a happier place and wars might never happen.

At school he often left his body sitting

at its desk while his mind went off on its journeys, and even at home daydreaming could sometimes get him into trouble. One Christmas Peter's father, Thomas Fortune, was hanging the decorations in the living room. It was a job he hated. It always put him in a bad mood. He was wanting to tape some streamers high in one corner. Now, in that corner was an armchair, and sitting in that armchair doing nothing in particular was Peter.

"Don't move, Pete," said Mr. Fortune. "I'm going to stand on the back of your chair to reach up here."

"That's fine," Peter said. "You go ahead."

Up onto the chair went Thomas Fortune, and away in his thoughts went Peter. He looked like he was doing nothing, but in fact he was very busy. He was inventing an exciting way of coming down a mountain quickly using a coat hanger and a length of wire stretched

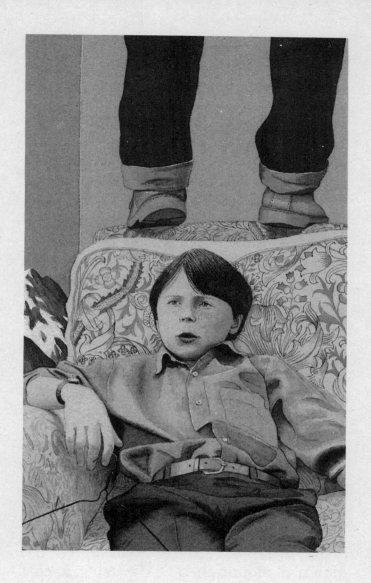

tight between the pine trees. He went on thinking about this problem while his father stood on the back of his chair, straining and gasping as he reached up to the ceiling. How, Peter wondered, would you go on sliding down without slamming into the trees that were holding up the wire?

Perhaps it was the mountain air that made Peter remember he was hungry. In the kitchen was an unopened box of chocolate cookies. It was a pity to go on neglecting them. Just as he stood up, there was a terrible crash behind him. He turned just in time to see his father fall headfirst into the gap between the chair and the corner. Then Thomas Fortune reappeared, headfirst again, looking ready to chop Peter into tiny bits. On the other side of the room Peter's mother clamped her hand across her mouth to hide her laughter.

"Oh, sorry, Dad," Peter said. "I forgot you were there."

Not long after his tenth birthday Peter was entrusted with the mission of taking his seven-year-old sister, Kate, to school. Peter and Kate went to the same school. It was a fifteen-minute walk or a short bus ride away. Usually they walked there with their father, who dropped them off on his way to work. But now the children were thought old enough to make it to school by themselves on the bus, and Peter was in charge.

It was only two stops down the road, but the way his parents kept going on about it, you might have thought Peter was taking Kate to the North Pole. He was given instructions the night before. When he woke up he had to listen to them over again. Then his parents repeated them all through breakfast. As the children were on their way out the door, their mother, Viola Fortune, ran through the rules one last time. "Everyone must think I'm stupid," Peter thought. "Perhaps I am." He was to keep hold of Kate's hand at all times. They were to sit close to the front, with Kate nearest the window. They were not to get into conversations with lunatics. Peter was to tell the bus driver the name of his stop in a loud voice, without forgetting to say please. He was to keep his eyes on the route.

Peter repeated all this back to his mother and set off for the bus stop with his sister. They held hands all the way. Actually he didn't mind this because the truth was, he really liked Kate. He simply hoped that none of his friends would see him holding a girl's hand. The bus came. They got on and sat close to the front. It was ridiculous sitting there holding hands, and there were some boys from school there, so they let go of each other. Peter was feeling proud of himself. He could take care of his sister anywhere. She could count on him. If they were alone together on a mountain pass and came face to face with a pack of hungry wolves, he would know exactly what to do. Taking care not to make any sudden movement, he would move away with Kate until they had their backs to a large rock. That way the wolves would not be able to surround them. Then he takes from his pocket two important things he has remembered to bring with him: his hunting knife and a box of matches. He takes the knife from its sheath and sets it down on the grass, ready in case the wolves attack. They are coming closer now. They are so hungry, they are drooling and growling and baying. Kate is crying, but he cannot comfort her. He knows he has to concentrate on his plan. Right at their feet are some dry leaves and twigs. Quickly and skillfully Peter gathers them into a small pile. The wolves are edging closer. He has to get this right. There is only one match left in the box. They can smell the wolves' breath—a terrible rotten-meat stench. He bends down, cups his hand, and lights the match. There is a gust of wind, the flame flickers, but Peter holds it close to the pile, and then first one leaf, then another, then the end of a twig catch fire, and soon the little pile is blazing. He piles on more leaves and twigs and larger sticks. Kate is getting the idea and helping him. The wolves are backing off. Wild animals are terrified of fire. The flames are leaping higher and the wind is carrying the smoke right into their slobbering jaws. Now Peter takes hold of the hunting knife and—

Ridiculous! It was daydreams like this could make him miss his stop if he wasn't careful. The bus had come to a halt. The kids from his school were already getting off. Peter leaped to his feet and just managed to jump to the pavement as the bus was starting off again. It was more than fifty yards down the road when he realized he had forgotten something. Was it his backpack? No! It was his sister! He had saved her from the wolves and left her sitting there. For a moment he couldn't move. He stood watching the bus pull away up the road. "Come back," he murmured. "Come back."

One of the boys from his school came over and thumped him on the back.

"Hey, what's up? Seen a ghost?"

Peter's voice seemed to come from far away. "Oh, nothing, nothing. I left something on the bus." And then he started to run. The bus was already a quarter of a mile away and beginning to slow down for its next stop. Peter sprinted. He was going so fast that if he spread his arms far apart, he would probably have been able to take off. Then he could skim along the top of the trees and— But no! He wasn't going to start daydreaming again. He was going to get his sister back. Even now she would be screaming in terror.

Some passengers had got off, and now the bus was moving away again. He was closer than before, and the traffic was heavy. The bus was crawling behind a truck. If he could just keep running and forget the terrible pain in his legs and chest, he would catch up. When he drew level with the bus stop, the bus was no more than a hundred yards away. "Faster, faster," he said to himself.

There was a kid standing by the bus shelter who called out to Peter as he passed. "Hey, Peter. Peter!"

Peter didn't have the strength to turn his head. "Can't stop," he panted, and ran on.

"Peter! Stop! It's me, Kate!"

Clutching at his chest, Peter collapsed on the grass at his sister's feet.

"Look out for that dog mess," she said

calmly as she watched her brother fighting for his breath. "Come on now. We better walk back or else we are going to be late. You'd better hold my hand if you're going to stay out of trouble."

So they walked to school together, and Kate very decently promised—in return for Peter's Saturday allowance—to say nothing about what had happened when they got home.

The trouble with being a daydreamer who doesn't say much is that the teachers at school, especially the ones who don't know you very well, are likely to think you are stupid. Or if not stupid, then dull. No one can see the amazing things that are going on inside your head. A teacher who saw Peter staring out the window or at a blank sheet of paper on his desk might think that he was bored or stuck for an answer. But the truth was quite different.

For example, one morning the children in Peter's class were given a math test. They had to add up some very large numbers, and they had twenty minutes. Almost as soon as he had started on the first sum, which involved adding three million five hundred thousand, two hundred and ninety-five to another number almost as large, Peter found himself thinking about the largest number in the world. He had read the week before about a number with the wonderful name of googol. A googol was ten multiplied by ten a hundred times. Ten with a hundred zeros on the end. And there was an even better word, a real beauty: googolplex. A googolplex was ten multiplied by ten a googol number of times. What a number!

Peter let his mind wander off into the fantastic size of it. The zeros trailed into space like bubbles. His father had told him that astronomers had worked out that the total number of atoms in all the millions of stars they could see through their giant telescopes was ten with ninety-eight zeros on the end. All the atoms in the world did not even add up to one single googol. And a googol was the tiniest little scrap of a thing compared to a googolplex. If you asked someone for a googol of chocolate-covered toffees, there wouldn't be nearly enough atoms in the universe to make them.

Peter propped his head on his hand and sighed. At that very moment the teacher clapped her hands. Twenty minutes were up. All Peter had done was write out the first number of the first sum. Everyone else had finished. What the teacher had been seeing all this time was Peter staring at his page, writing nothing and sighing.

Not long after that he was put with a group of children who had great difficulty adding up even small numbers like four and six. Quite soon Peter really did become bored and found it even harder to pay attention. The teachers began to think he was too bad at math even for this special group. What were they to do with him?

Of course Peter's parents and his sister, Kate, knew that Peter wasn't stupid or lazy or bored, and there were teachers at his school who came to realize that all sorts of interesting things were happening in his mind. And Peter himself learned as he grew older that since people can't see what's going on in your head, the best thing to do, if you want them to understand you, is to tell them. So he began to write down some of the things that happened to him when he was staring out of the window or lying on his back looking up at the sky. When he grew up, he became an inventor and a writer of stories and led a happy life. In this book you will find some of the weird adventures that happened in Peter's head, written down exactly as they happened.

CHAPTER TWO

THE DOLLS

EVER SINCE he could remember, Peter had shared a bedroom with Kate. Most of the time he did not mind. She made him laugh. And there were nights when Peter woke from a nightmare and was glad to have someone else in the room, even if it was his seven-year-old sister, who would be no use against the red-skinned, slime-covered creatures who chased him through his sleep. When he woke up, these monsters slid behind the curtains or crept into the closet. Because Kate was in the room, it was just that little bit easier to get out of bed and sprint across the landing to his parents' room.

But there were times when he did mind sharing a room. And Kate minded too. There were long afternoons when they got on each other's nerves. A squabble would lead to an argument, and an argument to a fight, a proper punching, scratching, hair-pulling fight. Since Peter was three years older, he expected to win these all-out battles. And in a sense he did. He could always count on making Kate cry first.

But was this really winning? Kate could hold her breath and push and make her face the color of a ripe plum. All she needed to do then was run downstairs

and show her mother "what Peter did."
Or she might lie on the floor making a
rattling sound in her throat so that Peter
thought she was about to die. Then *he*
would have to run down the stairs to
fetch Mom. Kate could also scream.
Once, during one of her noise storms, a
car passing the house had stopped and a
worried man had got out and stared up at
the bedroom window. Peter was looking
out at the time. The man ran up the garden and hammered on the door. He was
certain something terrible was happening inside. And it was. Peter had borrowed something of Kate's, and she
wanted it back. *Now!*

On all these occasions Peter was the
one who got into trouble, and Kate was
the one who came out on top. At least
this was how Peter saw it. When he got
angry with Kate, he had to think carefully before hitting her. Often they kept
the peace by drawing an imaginary line

from the door right across their bedroom. Kate's side there, Peter's side here. On this side, Peter's drawing and painting table, his one soft toy, a giraffe with a bent neck, the chemistry and electricity and printing sets that were never as much fun as the pictures on the box lids promised, and the tin trunk he kept his secrets in, which Kate was always trying to open.

Over there was Kate's painting and drawing table, her telescope, microscope, and magnetism sets, which *were* as much fun as the pictures on their lids promised, and everywhere else in her half of the room were the dolls. They sat along the window ledge with their legs dangling idly, they balanced on her chest of drawers and flopped over its mirror, they sat in a toy baby carriage, jammed like train commuters. The ones in favor crept nearer her bed. They were all colors, from shiny boot-polish black to deathly white, though most were a glowing pink. Some were naked, others wore only one item, a sock, a T-shirt, a bonnet, and a few were dressed to the nines in ball gowns with sashes, lace-trimmed frocks, and long skirts trailing ribbons. They were all quite different, but they all had one thing in common: they all had the same wide, mad, unblinking angry stare. They were meant to be babies, but their eyes gave them away. Babies never looked at anyone like that. When he walked past the dolls, Peter felt watched, and when he was out of the room, he had the idea they were talking about him, all sixty of them.

Still, they never did Peter any harm, and there was only one that he really disliked. The Bad Doll. Even Kate did not like it. She was scared of it, so scared that she did not dare throw it out in case it came back in the middle of the night and took its revenge. You would know

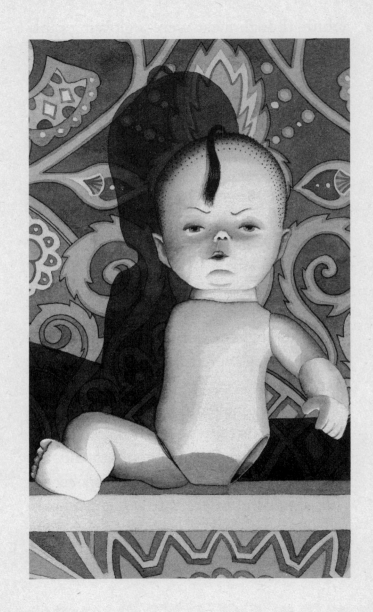

the Bad Doll at a glance. It was a pink
that no human had ever been. Long ago
its left leg and its right arm had been
wrenched from their sockets, and from
the top of its pitted skull grew one thick
hank of black hair. Its makers had wanted
to give it a sweet little smile, but something must have gone wrong with the
mold, because the Bad Doll always curled
its lips in scorn and frowned, as if trying
to remember the nastiest thing in the
world.

Of all the dolls, only the Bad Doll was
neither boy nor girl. The Bad Doll was
simply "it." It was naked, and it sat as far
as possible from Kate's bed where it
looked down on the others. Kate sometimes took it in her hands and tried to
soothe it with her murmurs, but it was
never long before she shuddered and
quickly put it back.

The imaginary line in their bedroom
worked well when they remembered

about it. They had to ask permission to cross to the other's half. Kate was not to pry into Peter's secret trunk, and Peter was not to touch Kate's microscope without asking first. It worked well enough, until one wet Sunday afternoon they had a fight, one of their worst, about exactly where this line was. Peter was sure it was farther away from his bed. This time Kate did not need to turn purple, or pretend to die, or scream. She clocked Peter on the nose with the Bad Doll. She had it by its one fat pink leg and swung it at his face. So it was Peter who went running downstairs crying. His nose was not actually hurting that much, but it was bleeding and he wanted to make the most of it. As he hurried down, he smeared the blood all over his face with the back of his hand, and when he came into the kitchen, he fell to the floor in front of his mother and wailed and moaned and writhed. Sure enough,

Kate got into trouble, big trouble.

This was the fight that made their parents decide it was time Peter and Kate had separate rooms. Not long before Peter's tenth birthday his father cleared out what was called the "box room" even though it contained no boxes, only old picture frames and broken armchairs. Peter helped his mother decorate the room. They hung curtains and squeezed in a huge iron bed with brass knobs on it.

Kate was so happy, she helped Peter carry his stuff across the landing. No more fights. And she would no longer have to listen to the disgusting gurgling, piping noise her brother made in his sleep. And Peter could not stop singing. Now he had a place where he could go and, well, just *be*. That night he chose to go to bed half an hour early in order to enjoy his own place, his own things, with no imaginary line down the middle of the room. He lay in the semidarkness and thought that it was just as well some good at last had come from that vile monstrosity the Bad Doll.

So the months passed, and Peter and Kate became used to having their own rooms and no longer gave it much thought. The interesting dates came and went: Peter's birthday, Christmas, Kate's birthday, and then Easter. It was two days after the traditional family Easter egg hunt, and Peter was in his room, sitting on his bed, about to eat his last egg. It was the biggest, the heaviest, which was why he had saved it until last. He peeled off the silver and blue foil wrapper. It was almost the size of a soccer ball. He held it in two hands, gazing at it. Then he drew it toward him and pushed into the shell with his thumbs. How he loved the thick, buttery cocoa aroma that poured from the dark hollowness inside. He raised the egg to his nose and breathed in. Then he started to eat.

Outside it was raining. There was still a week of vacation. Kate was out at a friend's house. There was nothing to do but eat. Twenty minutes later all that was left of the egg was the wrapper and the brightly colored box. Peter got to his feet, swaying slightly. He felt sick and bored, a perfect combination for a wet afternoon. How strange it was that having his own room was not exciting anymore. "Sick of chocolate," he sighed as he went toward his door. "Sick of my room!"

He stood on the landing, wondering if he was about to be sick. But instead of heading to the bathroom, he walked toward Kate's room and stepped inside. He had been back hundreds of times before, of course, but never alone. He stood in the center of the room, watched, as usual, by the dolls. He felt peculiar, and everything looked different. The room was bigger, and he had never noticed before how the floor sloped. There seemed to be more dolls than ever with their glassy stares, and as he went down the slope toward his old bed, he thought he heard a sound, a rustling. He thought he saw something move, but when he turned, everything was still.

He sat on his bed and thought back over the old days when he had slept here. He'd been just a kid then. Nine! What could he have known? If only his ten-year-old self could go back and tell that innocent fool what was what. When you got to ten, things began to fall into place, you began to see the whole picture, how things connected, how things worked, an overview. . . .

Peter was so intent on trying to re-member his ignorant younger self of six months before that he did not notice the figure making its way across the carpet toward him. When he did, he gave a shout of surprise and scrambled right onto the bed and drew up his knees.

Coming toward him at an awkward but steady pace was the Bad Doll. It had taken a paintbrush from Kate's desk to use as a crutch. It hobbled across the room with bad-tempered gasps, and it was muttering swear words that even a bad doll should not use. It stopped by the bedpost to get its breath. Peter was surprised to notice how sweaty its forehead and upper lip were. The Bad Doll leaned the paintbrush against the bed and drew its only forearm across its face. And then, with a quick glance at Peter and taking a deep breath, the Bad Doll snatched up its crutch and set about climbing onto the bed.

Scrambling up three times your own height with one arm and one leg takes patience and strength. The Bad Doll had little of either. Its little pink body quivered with the effort and strain as it hung halfway up the post, looking for leverage for its paintbrush. The gasps and grunts became louder and more piteous. Slowly its head, sweatier than ever, rose into Peter's view. He could easily have reached over and lifted the creature onto the bed. And just as easily he could have swatted it to the floor. But he did nothing. It was all so interesting. He just wanted to see what would happen. As the Bad Doll inched its way up with cries of "Oh, blast and hell's teeth!" and "Damnation take the grit!" and "Filthy custard!" Peter became aware that the head of every doll in the room was turned in his direction. Pure blue eyes blazed wider than ever, and there was a soft whispering of sibilants like water tumbling over rocks, a sound that gathered into a murmur and then a torrent, as excitement swept through five dozen spectators.

"He's doing it!" Peter heard one of them call.

And another answered, "Now we'll see something!"

And yet another called out, "What's fair is fair!" and at least twenty dolls shouted their agreement.

"Yes!"

"That's right!"

"Well put!"

The Bad Doll had got its arm onto the bed and had let go of its crutch. Now it was clawing at the blanket, trying to get a grip so it could pull itself up. And even as it was doing this, on the other side of the room there arose an almighty cheer, and suddenly the dolls, all the dolls, were making their way toward the bed. From windowsills and from on top of the mirror, from Kate's bed and from out of the toy baby carriage they came springing and leaping, spilling and tumbling and surging across the carpet. Dolls in long dresses shrieked as they stumbled and tripped, while naked dolls and one-sock dolls moved with horrible ease. On they came, a wave of brown and pink and black and white, and on every pouting lip was the cry "What's fair is fair! What's fair is fair!" And in every wide glassy eye was the anger that Peter had always suspected behind the pretty baby blue.

The Bad Doll had made it onto the bed and was standing, exhausted but proud, waving to the crowd gathered below. The dolls pressed tight together and roared their approval and raised their chubby, dimpled arms toward their leader.

"What's fair is fair!" The chant began again.

Peter had moved down to the far end of the bed. His back was to the wall, and his arms were clasped around his knees. This really was extraordinary. Surely his mother would hear the racket downstairs and come up to tell them to be quiet.

The Bad Doll needed to catch its breath, so it was letting the chant go on. Then it picked up the paintbrush crutch and the dolly rabble was suddenly silent.

With a wink for the benefit of its supporters the lame doll hopped a pace or two closer to Peter and said, "Settled in nicely, have you?" Its tone was very polite, but there were titters in the crowd, and Peter suspected he was being teased.

"I'm not sure what you mean," he said.

The Bad Doll turned to the crowd and did a good imitation of Peter's voice. "He's not sure what I mean." It turned back to Peter. "I mean, comfortable in your new room, are you?"

"Oh, that," Peter said. "Yes, my room is terrific."

Some of the dolls down on the carpet seized on this word and repeated it over and over again. "Terrific, terrific,

terrific," until it began to sound like a very stupid word indeed, and Peter wished he had not used it.

The Bad Doll waited patiently. When the crowd was quiet again, it asked, "Like having your own room, do you?"

"I do," Peter replied.

"Like having a room all to yourself."

"Yes, I just told you, I like it," Peter said.

The Bad Doll limped one pace closer. Peter had the feeling that it was about to come to the point. It raised its voice. "And have you ever considered that someone else might want that room?"

"That's ridiculous," Peter said. "Mom and Dad share a room. That leaves only Kate and me—"

His words were drowned out by a roar of disapproval from the crowd. The Bad Doll managed to balance on one leg while it raised its crutch in the air for silence.

"Only two of you, eh?" it said, nodding toward the crowd.

Peter laughed. He couldn't think of what to say.

The Bad Doll came even closer. Peter could have reached out and touched it. He was sure he could smell chocolate on its breath.

"Don't you think," it said, "that it's time someone else had a turn in that room?"

"That's ridiculous," Peter started to say. "You're only dolls—"

Nothing could have made the Bad Doll more furious. "You've seen how we live," it screamed. "Sixty of us squashed into one corner of the room. You've passed us a thousand times, and you've never given it a thought. What do you care that we're piled on top of each other like bricks in a wall. You just don't see what's in front of you. Look at us! No space, no privacy, not even a bed for most of us. Now it's someone else's turn with that room. What's fair is fair!"

Another great roar went up from the crowd, and once again the chant was taken up. "What's fair is fair! What's fair is fair!" And as it was bellowed out, the dolls began to swarm up onto the bed, standing on each other's shoulders to make ladders of their bodies. Within a minute the whole crew stood panting before Peter, and the Bad Doll, who had retreated to the far end of the bed, waved its crutch from the back of the crowd and shouted, "Now!"

Sixty pairs of chubby hands took hold of Peter's left leg.

"Yo-ho heave-ho!" sang out the Bad Doll.

"Yo-ho heave-ho!" answered the crowd.

And then a strange thing happened. Peter's leg came off. It came right off. He looked down at where his leg used to be, and instead of blood there was a little coiled spring poking out through his torn trousers.

"That's funny," he thought. "I never would have guessed . . ."

But he did not have much time to think about how funny it was because now the dolls had grabbed his right arm and were pulling and yo-ho heave-hoing, and his arm was off too, and sticking out from his shoulder was another little spring.

"Hey!" Peter shouted. "Give me back my arm and leg."

But it was no use. The arm and leg were being passed over the heads in the crowd, back toward the Bad Doll. It took the leg and slotted it on. A perfect fit. Now it was putting the arm in place. That arm could have been made specially, it fit so well.

"Odd," Peter thought. "I'm sure my arm and leg would be too big."

Even as he was thinking this, the dolls

were on him again, and this time they were scrambling up his chest, pulling his hair, ripping at his clothes.

"Get off," Peter shouted. "Ouch! That hurts."

The dolls laughed as they yanked out nearly all his hair. They left one long hank sticking out of the middle of his head.

The Bad Doll tossed Peter its crutch and leaped up and down to test its new leg. "My turn for that room," it called. "And as for him, he can go up there." It pointed, with what Peter still thought of as *his* arm, at the bookcase. The Bad Doll leaped nimbly to the floor, and the crowd swept forward to seize Peter and carry him off to his new home. And that is how it would have ended. But just then Kate stepped into the room.

Now, you have to try and imagine how it looked from where she stood. She had come home from playing with her friend, she had walked into her bedroom, and there was her brother, lying on the spare bed, playing with her dolls, *all* her dolls, and he was moving them around and doing their voices. The only one not on the bed was the Bad Doll, who was lying on the carpet nearby.

Kate could have got angry. After all, this was against all their rules. Peter was in her room without her permission, *and* he had taken down all her dolls from their special places. But instead Kate laughed to see her brother with sixty dolls piled on top of him.

Peter stood up quickly as soon as he saw Kate. He was blushing.

"Oh . . . er . . . sorry," he mumbled, and he tried to edge past her.

"Wait a minute," Kate said. "What about putting them back. They all have their own places, you know."

So, while Kate told him where they belonged, Peter put every single doll back in its place, on the mirror, the chest of drawers, the windowsills, the bed, the baby carriage.

It seemed to take forever to get them all in place. The very last to be returned was the Bad Doll. As Peter set it down on top of the bookcase, he was sure he heard it say, "One day, my friend, that room will be mine."

"Oh, damnation take the grit!" Peter whispered to it. "You filthy mustard!"

"What did you say?" Kate called out. But her brother had already stepped out of the room.

CHAPTER THREE

THE CAT

WHEN PETER woke in the morning, he always kept his eyes closed until he had answered two simple questions. They always came to him in the same order. Question one: Who am I? Oh, yes. Peter, aged ten. Then, still with his eyes closed, question two: What day of the week is it? And there it would be, a fact as solid and immovable as a mountain. Tuesday. Another school day. Then he would pull the blankets over his head and sink deeper into his own warmth and let the friendly darkness swallow him up. He could almost pretend he did not exist. But he knew he would have to force himself out. The whole world agreed it was Tuesday. The earth itself, hurtling through cold space, spinning and revolving around the sun, had brought everyone to Tuesday and there was nothing Peter, his parents, or the government could do to change the fact. He would have to get up or miss his bus and be late and get into trouble.

How cruel it was then to drag his warm dozy body from its nest and grope for his clothes, knowing that in less than an hour he would be shivering at the bus stop. On television the weatherman had said that it was the coldest winter in fifteen years. Cold, but no fun. No snow, no frost, not even an icy puddle to skate on. Only cold and gray, with a bitter wind that reached into Peter's bedroom through a crack in the window. There were times when it seemed to him that all he had ever done in his life, and all he was ever going to do, was wake up, get up, and go to school. It did not make it easier that everyone else, grown-ups included, had to get up on dark winter mornings. If only they would all agree to stop, then he could stop too. But the earth kept turning, Monday, Tuesday, Wednesday came around again, and everyone went on getting out of bed.

The kitchen was a kind of halfway house between his bed and the big world outside. Here the air was thick with toast smoke, kettle steam, and bacon smells. Breakfast was meant to be a family meal, but it rarely happened that all four of them sat down at once. Both Peter's parents went out to work, and there was always someone running around the table in a panic, looking for a lost paper or an appointment book or a shoe, and you had to grab whatever was cooking on the stove and find a place for yourself.

It was warm in here, almost as warm as bed, but it was not as peaceful. The air was filled with accusations disguised as questions.

"Who's fed the cat?"

"What time are you coming home?"

"Did you finish that homework?"

"Who's had my briefcase?"

As the minutes passed, the confusion and urgency increased. It was a family rule that the kitchen had to be tidied before anyone left the house. Sometimes you had to snatch your piece of bacon from the frying pan before it was tipped into the cat's bowl and the pan plunged into the washing-up water. The four members of the family ran backward and forward with dirty plates and cereal boxes, bumping into each other, and there was always someone muttering, "I'm going to be late, I'm going to be late. Third time this week!"

But there was in fact a fifth member of the household who was never in a rush and who ignored the commotion. He lay stretched out on a shelf on top of the radiator, eyes half closed, his only sign of life an occasional yawn. It was an enormous yawn, an insulting yawn. The mouth opened wide to show a clean pink tongue, and when at last it closed again, a comfortable shudder rippled from whiskers to tail: William the cat was settling down to his day.

When Peter snatched up his backpack and took one last look around before running out of the house, it was always William he saw. His head was cushioned on one paw, while the other dangled carelessly over the edge of the shelf, dabbling in the rising warmth. Now that the ridiculous humans were leaving, a cat could get in a few hours of serious snoozing. The image of the dozing cat tormented Peter as he stepped out of the house into the icy blast of the north wind.

If you believe it is strange to think of a cat as a real member of a family, then you should know that William's age was greater than Peter's and Kate's together. As a young cat he knew their mother when she was still at school. He had gone with her to college and five years later had been present at her wedding reception. When Viola Fortune was expecting her first baby and rested in bed some afternoons, William Cat used to drape himself over the big round hump in her middle that was Peter. At the births of both Peter and Kate he had disappeared from the house for days on end. No one knew where or why he went. He had

quietly observed all the sorrows and joys
of family life. He had watched the babies
become toddlers who tried to carry him
about by the ears, and he had seen the
toddlers turn into schoolchildren. He had
known the parents when they were a
wild young couple living in one room.
Now they were less wild in their three-
bedroom house. And William Cat was
less wild too. He no longer brought mice
or birds into the house to lay them at the
feet of ungrateful humans. Soon after his
fourteenth birthday he gave up fighting
and no longer proudly defended his territory. Peter thought it outrageous that a
bully of a young tom from next door was
taking over the garden, knowing that
old William could not do a thing about
it. Sometimes the tom came through
the cat flap into the kitchen and ate
William's food while the old cat watched
helplessly. And only a few years before,
no sensible cat would have dared set a

paw upon the lawn.

William must have been sad about the loss of his powers. He gave up the company of other cats and sat alone in the house with his memories and reflections. But despite his seventeen years he kept himself sleek and trim. He was mostly black, with dazzling white socks and shirt front and a splash of white on the tip of his tail. Sometimes he would seek you out where you were sitting, and after a moment's thought jump onto your lap and stand there, feet splayed, gazing deeply without blinking into your eyes. Then he might cock his head, still holding your gaze, and miaow, just once, and you would know he was telling you something important and wise, something you would never understand.

There was nothing Peter liked better on a winter's afternoon when he came home from school than to kick off his shoes and lie down beside William Cat in front of the living room fire. He liked to get right down to William's level and put his face up close to the cat's and see how extraordinary it really was, how beautifully nonhuman, with spikes of black hair sprouting in a globe from a tiny face beneath the fur, and the white whiskers with their slight downward curve, and the eyebrow hairs shooting up like radio antennae, and the pale-green eyes with their upright slits, like doors ajar into a world Peter could never enter. As soon as he came close to the cat, the deep rumbling purr would begin, so low and strong that the floor vibrated. Peter knew he was welcome.

It was just one such afternoon, a Tuesday as it happened, four o'clock and already the light fading, curtains drawn and lights on, when Peter eased himself onto the carpet where William lay before a bright fire whose flames were curling around a fat elm log. Down the chimney came the moan of the freezing wind as it whipped across the rooftops. Peter had sprinted from the bus stop with Kate to keep warm. Now he was safely indoors with his old friend, who was pretending to be younger than his years by rolling onto his back and letting his front paws flop helplessly. He wanted his chest tickled. As Peter began to move his fingers lightly through the fur, the rumbling noise grew louder, so loud that every bone in the old cat's body rattled. And then William stretched out a paw to Peter's fingers and tried to draw them up higher. Peter let the cat guide his hand.

"Do you want me to tickle your chin?" he murmured. But no. The cat wanted to be touched right at the base of his throat. Peter felt something hard there. It moved from side to side when he touched it. Something had got trapped in the fur. Peter propped himself on an elbow in order to investigate. He parted the fur. At first he thought he was looking at a piece of jewelry, a little silver tag. But there was no chain, and as he poked and peered, he saw that it was not metal at all but polished bone, oval and flattened in the center, and most curious of all, that it was attached to William Cat's skin. The piece of bone fitted well between his forefinger and thumb. He tightened his grip and gave a tug. William Cat's purr grew even louder. Peter pulled again, downward, and this time he felt something give.

Looking down through the fur and parting it with the tips of his fingers, he saw that he had opened up a small slit in the cat's skin. It was as if he were holding the handle of a zipper. Again he pulled, and now there was a dark opening two inches long. William Cat's purr was coming from in there. "Perhaps," Peter thought, "I'll see his heart beating."

A paw was gently pushing against his fingers again. William Cat wanted him to go on.

And this is what he did. He unzipped the whole cat from throat to tail. Peter wanted to part the skin to peep inside. But he did not want to appear nosy. He was just about to call out to Kate when there was a movement, a stirring inside the cat, and from the opening in the fur there came a faint pink glow that grew brighter. And suddenly out of William Cat climbed a, well, a thing, a creature. But Peter was not certain that it was really there to touch, for it seemed to be made entirely of light. And although it did not have whiskers or a tail or a purr, or even fur or four legs, everything about it seemed to say *cat*. It was the very essence of the word, the heart of the idea. It was a quiet, slinky, curvy fold of pink and purple light, and it was climbing out of the cat.

"You must be William's spirit," Peter said aloud. "Or are you a ghost?"

The light made no sound, but it understood. It seemed to say, without actually speaking the words, that it was both these things and much more besides.

When it was clear of the cat, which continued to lie on its back on the carpet in front of the fire, the cat spirit drifted into the air and floated up to Peter's shoulder, where it settled. Peter was not frightened. He felt the glow of the spirit on his cheek. And then the light drifted behind his head, out of sight. He felt it touch his neck, and a warm shudder ran down his back. The cat spirit took hold of something knobbly at the top of his spine and drew it down, right down his back, and as his own body opened up, he felt the cool air of the room tickle the warmth of his insides.

It was the oddest thing, to climb out of your body, just step out of it and leave it

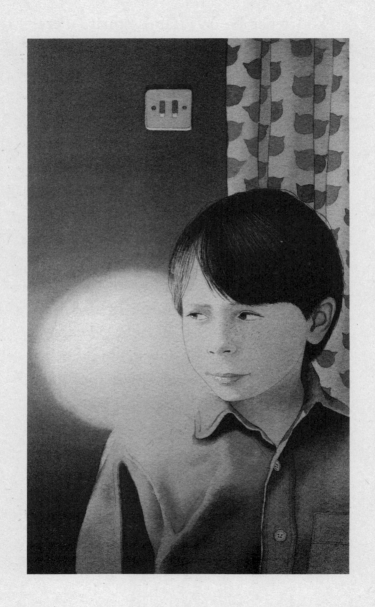

lying on the carpet like a shirt you had just taken off. Peter saw his own glow, which was purple and the purest white. The two spirits hovered in the air facing each other. And then Peter suddenly knew what he wanted to do, what he had to do. He floated toward William Cat and hovered. The body stood open, like a door, and it looked so inviting, so welcoming. He dropped down and stepped inside. How fine it was, to dress yourself as a cat. It was not squelchy, as he thought all insides must be. It was dry and warm. He lay on his back and slipped his arms into William's front legs. Then he wiggled his legs into William's back legs. His head fitted perfectly inside the cat's head. He glanced across at his own body just in time to see William Cat's spirit disappear inside.

Using his paws, Peter was able to zip himself up easily. He stood and took a few steps. What a delight, to walk on four soft white paws. He could see his whiskers springing out from the sides of his face, and he felt his tail curling behind him. His tread was light, and his fur was like the most comfortable of old woolen sweaters. As his pleasure in being a cat grew, his heart swelled, and a tingling sensation deep in his throat became so strong that he could actually hear himself. Peter was purring. He was Peter Cat, and over there was William Boy.

The boy stood up and stretched. Then, without a word to the cat at his feet, he skipped out of the room.

"Mom," Peter heard his old body call out from the kitchen. "I'm hungry. What's for supper?"

That night Peter was too restless, too excited, too much of a cat to sleep. Toward ten o'clock he slipped through the cat flap. The freezing night air could not penetrate his thick fur coat. He padded soundlessly across to the garden wall. It towered above him, but one effortless, graceful leap and he was up, surveying his territory. How wonderful it was to be able to see into dark corners, to feel every vibration of the night air on his whiskers, and to make himself invisible when, at midnight, a fox came up the garden path to root among the garbage cans. All around he was aware of other cats, some local, some from far away, going about their nighttime business, traveling their routes. After the fox, a young tabby tried to enter the garden. Peter warned him off with a hiss and a flick of his tail. He purred inwardly as the young fellow squealed in astonishment and took flight.

Not long after that, while patrolling the high wall that rose above the greenhouse, he came face to face with another cat, a more dangerous intruder. It was completely black, which was why Peter had not seen it sooner. It was the tom from next door, a vigorous fellow almost twice his size, with a thick neck and long powerful legs. Without even thinking Peter arched his back and upended his fur to make himself look big.

"Hey, puss," he hissed. "This is my wall and you're on it."

The black cat looked surprised. It smiled. "So it was your wall once, Grandpa. What'ya going to do about it now?"

"Beat it, before I throw you off." Peter was amazed at how strongly he felt. This *was* his wall, his garden, and it was his job to keep unfriendly cats out.

The black cat smiled again, coldly. "Listen, Grandpa. It hasn't been your wall for a long time. I'm coming through. Out of my way or I'll rip your fur off."

Peter stood his ground. "Take another step, you walking flea circus, and I'll tie your whiskers around your neck."

The black cat gave out a long laughing wail of contempt. But it did not take another step. All around, local cats were appearing out of the darkness to watch. Peter heard their voices.

"A fight?"

"A fight!"

"The old boy must be crazy!"

"He's seventeen if he's a day."

The black cat arched its powerful spine and howled again, a terrible rising note.

Peter tried to keep his voice calm, but his words came out in a hiss. "You don't take ssshort cuttsss through here without asssking me firssst."

The black cat blinked. The muscles in its fat neck rippled as it shrieked its laugh that was also a war cry.

On the opposite wall a moan of excitement ran through the crowd, which was still growing.

"Old Bill has flipped."

"He's chosen the wrong cat to pick a fight with."

"Listen, you toothless old sheep," the black cat said through a hiss far more penetrating than Peter's. "I'm number one around here. Isn't that right?"

The black cat half turned to the crowd, which murmured its agreement. Peter thought the watching cats did not sound very enthusiastic.

"My advice to you," the black cat went on, "is to step aside, or I'll spread your guts all over the lawn."

Peter knew he had gone too far now to back down. He extended his claws to take a firm grip on the wall. "You bloated rat! This is my wall, d'you hear? And you are nothing but the soft turd of a sick dog!"

The black cat gasped. There were titters in the crowd. Peter was always such a polite boy. How splendid it was now to spit out these insults.

"You'll be birds' breakfast," the black cat warned and took a step forward. Peter snatched a deep breath. For old William's sake he had to win. Even as he was thinking this, the black cat's paw lashed out at his face. Peter had an old cat's body, but he had a young boy's mind. He ducked and felt the paw and its vicious outstretched claws go singing through the air above his ears. He had time to see that the black cat was supported momentarily on only three legs. Immediately he sprang forward and with his two front paws pushed the tom hard in the chest. It was not the kind of thing a cat does in a fight and the number one cat was taken by surprise. With a yelp of astonishment he slipped and tottered backward, tipped off the wall, and fell headfirst through the roof of the greenhouse below. The icy night air was

shattered by the crash and musical tin-
kle of broken glass and the earthier
clatter of breaking flowerpots. Then
there was silence. The hushed crowd of
cats peered down from their wall. They
heard a bump, then a groan. Then, just
visible in the gloom was the shape of
the black cat hobbling across the lawn.
They heard it muttering.

"It's not fair. Claws and teeth, yes. But
pushing like that. It just isn't fair."

"Next time," Peter called down, "you
ask permission."

The black cat did not reply, but something about its retreating, limping shape
made it clear it had understood.

The next morning Peter lay on the
shelf above the radiator with his head
cushioned on one paw while the other
dangled loosely in the rising warmth. All
about him was hurry and chaos. Kate
could not find her backpack. The oatmeal
was burned. Thomas Fortune was in a

bad mood because the coffee had run out
and he needed three strong cups to start
his day. The kitchen was a mess and the
mess was covered in oatmeal smoke. And
it was late, late, late!

Peter curled his tail around his back
paws and tried not to purr too loudly. On
the far side of the room was his old body
with William Cat inside, and that body
had to go to school. William Boy was
looking confused. He had his coat on and
he was ready to leave, but he was wearing only one shoe. The other was
nowhere to be found. "Mom," he kept
bleating, "where's my shoe?" But Viola
Fortune was in the hallway arguing with
someone on the phone.

Peter Cat half closed his eyes. After
his victory he was desperately tired.
Soon the family would be gone. The
house would fall silent. When the radiator had cooled, he would wander upstairs
and find the most comfortable of the

beds. For old times' sake he would choose his own.

The day passed just as he had hoped. Dozing, lapping a saucer of milk, dozing again, munching through some tinned cat food that really was not as bad as it smelled—rather like shepherd's pie without the mashed potato. Then more dozing. Before he knew it, the sky outside was darkening and the children were home from school. William Boy looked worn out from a day of classroom and playground struggle. Boy-cat and cat-boy lay down together in front of the living room fire. It was most odd, Peter Cat thought, to be stroked by a hand that only the day before had belonged to him. He wondered if William Boy was happy with his new life of school and buses and having a sister and a mom and dad. But the boy's face told Peter Cat nothing. It was so hairless, whiskerless, and pink, with eyes so round that it was impossible to know what they were saying.

Later that evening Peter wandered up to Kate's room. As usual she was talking to her dolls, giving them a lesson in geography. From the fixed expression on their faces it was clear they were not much interested in the longest rivers in the world. Peter jumped onto her lap and she began to tickle him absentmindedly as she talked. If only she could have known that the creature on her lap was her brother. Peter lay down and purred. Kate was beginning to list all the capital cities she could think of. It was so exquisitely boring, just what he needed to get him off to sleep again. His eyes were already closed when the door crashed open and William Boy strode in.

"Hey, Peter," Kate said. "You didn't knock."

But her brother-cat paid no attention. He crossed the room, picked up her cat-brother roughly, and hurried away with him. Peter disliked being carried. It was undignified for a cat of his age. He tried to struggle, but William Boy only tightened his grip as he rushed down the stairs. "Ssh," he said. "We don't have much time."

William carried the cat into the living room and set him down.

"Keep still," the boy whispered. "Do what I tell you. Roll onto your back."

Peter Cat had little choice, for the boy had pinned him down with one hand and was searching in his fur with the other. He found the piece of polished bone and pulled downward. Peter felt the cool air reach his insides. He stepped out of the cat's body. The boy was reaching up behind his own neck and unzipping himself. Now the pink and purple light of a true cat slipped out of the boy's body. For a moment the two spirits, cat and human, faced each other, suspended above the carpet. Below them their bodies lay still, waiting, like taxis ready to move off with their passengers. There was a sadness in the air.

Though the cat spirit did not speak, Peter sensed what it was saying. "I must return," it said. "I have another adventure to begin. Thank you for letting me be a boy. I have learned so many things that will be useful to me in the time to come. But most of all, thank you for fighting my last battle for me."

Peter was about to speak, but the cat spirit was returning to its own body.

"There's very little time," it seemed to say, as the pink and purple light folded itself into the fur of the cat. Peter drifted toward his own body and slipped in around the back, at the top of the spine.

It felt rather odd at first. This body did not really fit him. When he stood up, he was shaky on his legs. It was like wearing a pair of boots four sizes too large. Perhaps his body had grown a little since he had last used it. It felt safer to lie down for a moment. As he did so, the cat, William Cat, turned and walked very slowly and stiffly out of the room without even a glance at him.

As Peter lay there, trying to get used to his old body, he noticed a curious thing. The fire was still curling around the same elm log. He glanced toward the window. The sky was darkening. It was not evening, it was still late afternoon. From the newspaper lying near a chair he could see that it was still Tuesday. And here was another curious thing. His sister, Kate, was running into the room, crying. And following her were his parents, looking very grim.

"Oh, Peter," his sister cried. "Something terrible has happened."

"It's William Cat," his mother explained. "I'm afraid he's—"

"Oh, William!" Kate's wail drowned her mother's words.

"He just walked into the kitchen," his father said, "and climbed onto his favorite shelf above the radiator, closed his eyes, and . . . died."

"He didn't feel a thing," Viola Fortune said reassuringly.

Kate continued to cry. Peter realized that his parents were watching him anxiously, waiting to see how he was going to take the news. Of all the family, he was the one who had been closest to the cat.

"He was seventeen," Thomas Fortune said. "He had a good innings."

"He had a good life," Viola Fortune said.

Peter stood up slowly. Two legs did not seem enough.

"Yes," he said at last. "He's gone on another adventure now."

The next morning they buried William at the bottom of the garden. Peter made a cross out of sticks, and Kate made a wreath out of laurel leaves and twigs. Even though they were all going to be late for school or work, the whole family went down to the graveside together. The children put on the final shovelfuls of earth. And it was just then that there rose through the ground and hovered in the air a shining ball of pink and purple light.

"Look!" Peter said, and pointed.

"Look at what?"

"Right there, right in front of you."

"Peter, what are you talking about?"

"He's daydreaming again."

The light drifted higher until it was level with Peter's head. It did not speak, of course. That would have been impossible. But Peter heard it all the same.

"Good-bye, Peter," it said as it began to fade before his eyes. "Good-bye, and thanks again."

CHAPTER FOUR

VANISHING CREAM

IN THE BIG UNTIDY kitchen there was a drawer. Of course there were many drawers, but when someone said, "The string is in the kitchen drawer," everyone understood. Chances were, the string would not be in the drawer. It was meant to be, along with a dozen other useful things that were never there:

screwdrivers, scissors, Scotch tape, thumbtacks, pencils. If you wanted one of these, you looked in the drawer first, then you looked everywhere else. What *was* in the drawer was hard to define: things that had no natural place, things that had no use but did not deserve to be thrown away, things that might be mended one day. So: batteries that still had a little life, nuts without their bolts, the handle of a precious teapot, a padlock without a key or a combination lock whose secret number was a secret to everyone, the dullest kind of marbles, foreign coins, a flashlight without a bulb, a single glove from a pair lovingly knitted by Granny before she died, a hot water bottle stopper, a cracked fossil. By some magic reversal everything spectacularly useless filled the drawer intended for practical tools. What could you *do* with a single piece of jigsaw? But on the other hand, did you dare throw it away?

Now and then the drawer was cleared out. Viola Fortune tipped the whole rattling ensemble into the garbage, and restocked with string, tape, scissors . . . Then, gradually, these precious items left in protest as the junk began to creep back in.

Sometimes, in moments of boredom, Peter opened the drawer hoping the objects would suggest an idea or a game. They never did. Nothing fitted, nothing related. If a million monkeys shook the drawer up for a million years, it was possible the contents might fall together into a radio. But it was certain that the radio would never work and never get thrown away. And there were other times, like this boring, hot Saturday afternoon, when nothing was going right. Peter wanted to build something, invent something, but he could not find any useful bits and the rest of the family would not help. All they wanted to do was laze around on the grass, pretending to sleep. Peter was fed up with them. The drawer seemed to stand for everything that was wrong with his family. What a mess! No wonder he could not think straight. No wonder he was always daydreaming. If he lived on his own, he would know where to find screwdrivers and string. If he were by himself, he would know where his thoughts were, too. How was he expected to make the great inventions that would change the world when his sister and his parents threw up these mountains of disorder?

On this particular Saturday afternoon Peter was reaching deeper toward the back of the drawer. He was looking for a hook, but he knew there was little hope. His hand closed around a greasy little spring that had fallen out of the garden clippers. He let it go. Behind it were packets of seeds, too old to plant, not old enough to throw away. "What a family,"

Peter thought, as he shoved his hand right to the back of the drawer. "Why aren't we like other people, with batteries in everything, and toys that work, and jigsaws and card games with all their pieces, and everything in the proper cupboard?" His hand closed around something cold. He drew out a small dark-blue jar with a black lid. On a white label was printed VANISHING CREAM. He stared at these words a long time, trying to grasp their meaning. Inside was a thick white cream whose surface was smooth. It had never been used. He poked the tip of his forefinger in. The substance was cold—not the hard, fiery cold of ice, but a round, silky, creamy cool. He withdrew his finger and yelped in surprise. His fingertip was gone. Completely vanished. He screwed on the lid and hurried upstairs to his room. He put the jar on a shelf, kicked clothes and toys aside so that he could sit on the floor with his back against the bed. He needed to think.

First he examined his forefinger. It was almost as short as his thumb. He felt the space where his missing piece of finger should have been. There was nothing. His fingertip was not simply invisible. It had melted away.

After half an hour of quiet thought Peter went to his window, which over-looked the back garden. The lawn looked like an outdoor version of the kitchen drawer. There were his parents lying facedown on blankets, half asleep, soaking up the sunshine. Between them lay Kate, who probably thought it looked grown-up to sunbathe. Surrounding the trio was the debris of their wasted Saturday afternoon—teacups, teapot, news-papers, half-eaten sandwiches, orange peel, empty yogurt cartons. He stared at his family resentfully. You could do nothing with these people, but neither could you throw them away. Or rather, well, perhaps . . . He took a deep breath, put the little blue jar in his pocket, and went downstairs.

Peter knelt down beside his mother. She murmured dozily.

"You should be careful of sunburn, Mom," Peter said kindly. "Would you like me to rub some cream on your back?"

Viola Fortune mumbled something that sounded like a yes. He took out the jar. It was difficult to unscrew the lid with a forefinger missing. He slipped on the single glove he had collected on his way through the kitchen. His mother's white back gleamed in the sunlight. Everything was ready.

There was no doubt in Peter's mind that he loved his mother dearly and that she loved him. She had taught him how to make toffee and how to read and write. She had once jumped out an airplane with a parachute, and she looked after him at home when he was ill. She was the only mother he knew who could stand on her head unsupported. But he had made his decision, and she had to go. He scooped out a dollop of cold cream on the end of his gloved finger. The glove did not disappear. The magic seemed to work only on living tissue. He let the blob fall right in the middle of his mother's back.

"Oh," she sighed, without much conviction. "That really is cold." Peter began to spread the cream evenly, and his mother immediately began to vanish. There was an unpleasant moment when her head and legs were still on the grass, with nothing in between. He quickly rubbed another fingerful across her head and ankles.

She was gone. The ground where she had lain was flattened, but even as he watched, the blades were straightening up.

Peter took the little blue jar over to his

father. "Looks like you're burning, Dad," Peter said. "Want me to rub some cream on?"

"No," his father said, without opening his eyes. But Peter had already dug out a fat blob and was spreading it across his father's shoulders. Now, there was no one in the world Peter loved as much as his father, except his mother. And it was as clear as sunlight that his father loved him. Thomas Fortune still kept a 500cc motorbike in the garage (another item that could not be thrown away), and he gave Peter rides on it. He had taught Peter how to whistle, how to do up his shoelaces in a special way, and how to throw people over his head. But Peter had made his decision, and his father had to go. This time he worked the cream from feet to head in less than a minute, and all that was left on the grass was Thomas Fortune's reading glasses.

Only Kate remained. She lay contentedly, facedown, between two vanished parents. Peter looked in the blue jar. Just enough left for one small person. He would have been slow to admit that he loved his sister. A sister was simply *there*, whether you wanted her or not. But she was fun to play with when she was in a good mood, and she had the kind of face that made you want to talk to her, and it probably was true that underneath it all he did love her, and she him. Still, he had made up his mind, and she had to go.

He knew it would be a mistake to ask Kate if she wanted cream rubbed on her back. She would immediately suspect a trick. Children were harder to fool than grown-ups. He ran his finger around the bottom of the jar and was just about to let a medium-size globule fall on her when she opened her eyes and saw his gloved hand.

"What are you doing?" she shrieked. She leaped up, knocking Peter's arm and causing the cream intended for her back to splatter over her head. She was on her feet, clawing at her scalp. "Mom, Dad, he's put muck on me," she wailed.

"Oh, no," Peter said. Kate's head, as well as her hands, were disappearing. And now she was running around the garden like a headless chicken, waving her shortened arms. She would have been screaming if she had had a mouth to scream with. "This is terrible," Peter thought as he started after her. "Kate! Listen to me. Stop!" But Kate had no ears. She kept on running in ever-widening circles, until she collided with the garden wall and bounced back into Peter's arms. "What a family!" he thought, as he smeared the last of the vanishing cream over Kate. What a relief it was when at last she was gone and there was peace in the garden.

First of all he wanted the place tidy. He collected the litter on the lawn and tipped it into the garbage—teapot, cups, and all, thereby saving on washing up. From now on the house was going to be run efficiently. He took a large plastic bag up to his bedroom and stuffed it with loose items. Everything left lying in his path was deemed rubbish: clothes on the floor, toys on the bed, extra pairs of shoes. He patrolled the house, gathering up loose objects that looked untidy. He dealt with his sister's and his parents' bedrooms by simply closing the doors. He stripped the living room of ornaments, cushions, framed photographs, and books. In the kitchen he cleared the shelves of plates, cookbooks, and jars of disgusting pickles. When he had finished his work at the end of the afternoon, there were eleven bags of household junk lined up by the garbage cans.

He made himself supper, a white sugar sandwich. Afterward he chucked his plate and knife into the rubbish. Then he strolled through the house, admiring the empty rooms. Now at last he could think straight, now at last he could set about inventing his inventions, as soon as he had found a pencil and a clean sheet of paper. The problem was that loose items like pencils were probably in one of the eleven bags of garbage. Never mind. Before the hard work started he would spend a few minutes in front of the TV. Television was not forbidden in the Fortune household, nor was it encouraged. The daily ration was one hour. More than that, Thomas and Viola Fortune believed, would rot the brain. They offered no medical evidence for this theory. It was six in the evening when Peter sat down in the armchair with a gallon of lemonade, a box of toffees, and a sponge cake. That night he watched a week's worth. It was just after one in the morning when he lurched to his feet and stumbled into the dark hallway. "Mom," he called, "I'm going to be sick." He stood over the toilet bowl waiting for the worst. It did not come. What did was more unpleasant. From upstairs came a sound that was difficult to describe. It was a kind of squeaking, flip-flopping, squelching footstep, as though a slimy creature were tiptoeing across a giant puddle of green jelly. Peter's sickness disappeared and terror took its place. He stood at the foot of the stairs. He turned on the light and peered up. "Dad," he croaked. "Dad?" No answer.

No use trying to sleep downstairs. There were no blankets, and he had thrown out all the cushions. He began to climb the stairs. Each step creaked and gave him away. His heartbeat was thudding in his ears. He thought he heard the sound again, but he could not be sure. He stopped and held his breath. Only hissing silence and his knocking heart. He edged up another three steps. If only Kate were

in her room, talking to her dolls. He was four steps from the landing. If there was a monster shuffling backward and forward through a puddle of jelly, it had stopped and was waiting for him. His bedroom door was six steps away. He counted to three and made a dash for it. He slammed his door behind him, bolted it, and leaned against it, waiting.

He was safe. His room looked bare and menacing. He got into bed with his clothes and shoes on, ready to climb out the window should the monster break his door down. That night Peter did not sleep, he ran. He ran through his dreams, down echoing halls, across a desert of stones and scorpions, down ice mazes, along a sloping pink, spongy tunnel with dripping walls. This was when he realized he was not being chased by the monster. He was running down its throat.

He woke with a start and sat up. Outside it was light. It was late morning, perhaps, or early afternoon. The day already had a used-up feel. He unbolted his door and stuck his head out. Silence. Emptiness. He opened the curtains in his room. Sunlight flooded in and he began to feel braver. Outside was birdsong, traffic noise, the sound of a lawn mower. When darkness returned, so too would the monster. What was needed, he thought, was a booby trap. If he was going to think straight and invent his inventions, then he had to settle the monster for good. He needed—let's see— twenty thumbtacks, a flashlight, something heavy on the end of a piece of string attached to a pole . . .

These thoughts brought him downstairs and into the kitchen. He pulled open the drawer. He was pushing aside a package of birthday cake candleholders that had half melted last time they were used when he noticed his forefinger. It was all there! It had grown back. The effects of the cream had worn off. He was just beginning to consider what this might mean when he felt a hand on his shoulder. The monster? No, Kate, all of her, all in one piece.

Peter started jabbering. "Thank goodness you're here. I need your help. I'm making a booby trap. You see, there's this thing—"

Kate was pulling on his hand. "We've been calling you for ages from the garden. And you've just been standing there, looking at the drawer. Come and see what we're doing. Dad's got an old lawn mower engine. We're going to make a *Hovercraft.*"

"A Hovercraft!"

Peter let himself be led outside. Cups, orange peel, newspapers, and his parents—unvanished.

"Come on," called his mother. "Come and help."

Thomas Fortune had a wrench in

his hand. "It just might work," he said, "with your help."

As Peter ran toward his parents, he wondered what day it was. Still Saturday? He decided not to ask.

CHAPTER FIVE

THE BULLY

THERE WAS A BULLY at Peter's school and his name was Barry Tamerlane. He didn't look like a bully. He wasn't a scruff, his face wasn't ugly, he didn't have a frightening leer or scabs on his knuckles, and he didn't carry dangerous weapons. He wasn't particularly big. Nor was he one of those small, wiry, bony types who turn out to be vicious fighters. At home he wasn't smacked like many bullies are, nor was he spoiled. His parents were kind but firm, and quite unsuspecting. His voice wasn't loud or hoarse, his eyes weren't hard and small, and he wasn't even very stupid. In fact, he was rather round and soft, though not quite a fatty, with glasses and a spongy pink face and silver braces on his teeth. He often wore a sad and helpless look, which appealed to some grown-ups and was useful when he had to talk himself out of trouble.

So what made Barry Tamerlane a successful bully? Peter had given this question a great deal of dreamy thought. His conclusion was that there were two reasons for Barry's success. The first was that he seemed to be able to move in the quickest way between wanting something and having it. If you were in the playground with a toy and Barry Tamerlane liked the look of it, he simply wrenched it from your hands. If he needed a pencil in class, he just turned around and "borrowed" yours. If there was a line, he would walk right to the front of it. If he was angry with you, he said so and then hit you very hard. The second reason for Tamerlane's success was that everyone was afraid of him. No one quite knew why. The very name Barry Tamerlane was enough to make you feel an icy hand reaching into your stomach. You were frightened of him because everyone else was. He was frightening because he had a reputation for being frightening. When you saw him coming, you got out of his way, and when he asked for your candy or your toys, you handed them over. That's what people did, so it seemed sensible to do the same.

Barry Tamerlane was a powerful boy about the school. No one was able to stop him from having what he wanted. He wasn't able to stop himself. He was a blind force. He sometimes seemed to Peter like a robot who was programmed to do whatever he had to do. How strange that he didn't mind being without friends or having everyone hating and avoiding him.

Of course Peter kept out of the bully's way, but he took a special interest in him. Barry Tamerlane was a mystery. On his eleventh birthday Barry invited a dozen boys from school to a party. Peter tried to get out of it, but his parents would not listen. They themselves liked Mr. and Mrs. Tamerlane, and so, by the terms of grown-up logic, Peter must surely like Barry.

The smiling birthday boy met his guests at the front door. "Hello, Peter! Thanks. Hey, Mom, Dad, look what my friend Peter has given me!"

That afternoon Barry was kind to all

his guests. He joined in the games and did not expect to win every time just because it was his birthday. He laughed with his parents and poured out drinks and helped clear away and wash the dishes. At one point Peter peeped into Barry's bedroom. There were books all over the place, a train set on the floor, an old teddy on the bed wedged against a pillow, a chemistry set, a computer game—it was a bedroom just like his own.

At the end of the afternoon Barry gave Peter a gentle punch on the arm and said, "See you tomorrow, Peter."

"So Barry Tamerlane leads a double life," Peter thought as he walked home. "Each morning, somewhere along the way from home to school, the boy turns into a monster, and at the end of the day the monster turns back into a boy." These thoughts led Peter into daydreams about potions and spells that transform people;

and then, in the weeks after the birthday party, he thought no more about it. It is a mystery in itself how we can get used to living with mysteries, and there were far greater puzzles in the universe than Barry Tamerlane.

One of these puzzles had been on Peter's mind a great deal lately. He had been walking along the corridor outside his classroom, on his way to the library, when two big girls from the high school walked by.

One of them was saying to her friend, "But how do you know you're not dreaming now? You might be dreaming that you're talking to me."

"Oh, well," the friend said. "I could just pinch myself and it would hurt and I'd wake up."

"But suppose," the first girl said, "suppose you were just dreaming that you pinched yourself, and you just dreamed that it hurt. Everything could be a dream and you would never know. . . ."

They turned the corner and were gone. Peter stopped to think. This was an idea he himself had half formed, but he had never put it quite so clearly. He looked about him. The library book in his hand, the bright, broad corridor, the ceiling lights, the classrooms off to the left and right, the children coming out of them— they might not be there at all. They might be no more than thoughts in his head. Right by him on the wall was a fire extinguisher. He put his hand out and touched it. The red metal was cool beneath his fingers. It was solid, real. How could it not be there? But then that was how it was in dreams—everything seemed to be real. It was only when you woke that you knew you had been dreaming. How was he to know he was not dreaming the fire extinguisher, dreaming the red, dreaming the feel of it?

The days passed and Peter thought

more about this problem. He was standing in the garden one afternoon when he realized that if he was just dreaming the world, then everything in it, and everything that happened in it, was caused by him. Far above him an airplane was beginning its descent. Sunlight flashed silver on its wings. The people up there who were straightening their seat backs and putting away their magazines could have no idea they were being dreamed by a boy on the ground. Did this mean that when a plane crashed it was his fault? What a terrible idea! But then, if that were so, there were no real plane crashes anyway. They were just dreams. Even so, he stared at the plane and wished hard that it would make it safely to the airport. It did.

One night, a couple of days later, Peter's mother came into his bedroom to kiss him good night. Just as her lips touched his cheek, he had another thought. If he was dreaming, what would happen to his mother when he woke up? Would there be another mother, more or less the same only real? Or someone completely different? Or no one at all? Viola Fortune was rather surprised when Peter put his arms around her neck and wouldn't let go.

As the days passed and Peter turned the problem over in his mind, he began to think it was probably true that his life was just a dream. There was something quite dreamlike about the way the children streamed into school in the mornings like a human river, and the way his teacher's voice floated around the classroom walls, and the way her skirt stirred as she moved across to the blackboard. And it was just like a dream, the way the teacher was suddenly standing over him and saying, "Peter, Peter? Are you listening? Are you daydreaming again?"

He tried to tell her the truth. "I think,"

he said very carefully, "I was *dreaming* about daydreaming."

The whole class laughed. It was lucky for Peter that Mrs. Burnett had a soft spot for him. She ruffled his hair and said, "Pay attention," as she walked back to the front of the classroom.

So this was how it came about that during playtime Peter was standing by himself at the edge of the playground. Anyone watching would have seen a boy standing by a wall, holding an apple, staring into space, doing nothing. In fact, Peter was thinking hard. He had been on the point of eating his apple when he had had another brilliant idea. A breakthrough. If life was a dream, then dying must be the moment when you woke up. It was so simple, it must be true. You died, the dream was over, you woke up. That's what people meant when they talked about going to heaven. It was like waking up. Peter smiled. He was about to reward himself with a bite of his apple when he glanced up and found himself looking into the round pink face of Barry Tamerlane, the school bully.

He was smiling, but he did not look happy. He was smiling because he wanted something. He had walked across the playground in a straight line toward Peter, cutting right through the games of football and hopscotch and skipping.

He held his hand out and said simply, "I want that apple," and smiled again. Silvery sunlight flashed on his braces.

Now, Peter was not a coward. He had once limped down a mountain in Wales with a twisted ankle without a word of complaint. And he had once run into a rough sea fully clothed to drag a lady's dog out of the surf. But he had no heart for fighting. He shrank from it. He was strong enough for his age, but he knew he could never win a fight because he could never bring himself to hit anyone really hard. When a fight broke out in the playground and all the kids gathered around, Peter felt sick in his stomach and weak in his legs.

"Come on," Barry Tamerlane said in a reasonable voice. "Hand it over, or I'll smash your face in."

Peter felt the numbness stealing up his body from his feet. His apple was yellow streaked with red. Its skin was a little slack because he had brought it into school a week ago and it had been sitting in his desk, filling it with a sweet, woody scent. Was it worth a smashed face? Surely not. But then again, could he give it away just because a bully had demanded it?

He looked at Barry Tamerlane. He had edged a little closer. His pink, round face was flushed. His glasses magnified his eyes. A little bubble of saliva clung between the rim of his braces and a front tooth. He was no bigger, and certainly no stronger, than Peter.

Already a few children, sensing that a drama was building up around Tamerlane's corner of the playground, were beginning to gather in a ragged circle.

"G-wan, Pete. Smash his face in!" someone said unhelpfully. Barry Tamerlane turned around and glared, and the boy slunk away to the back of the crowd.

"C'mon, Barry! C'mon, Bas!" other voices said.

Barry Tamerlane did not like being refused. He was getting ready to fight. He had withdrawn his hand and made a fist and turned sideways. His knees were bent slightly and he swayed from side to side. He seemed to know what he was doing.

More children were joining the circle. Peter heard the call go out across the playground: "A fight! A fight!" People were running in from all directions.

Peter's heart was thudding in his ears.

The last time he had been in this situation he had been a cat with a human trick up his furry sleeve. But this was not so simple. Playing for time, he transferred the apple from one hand to the other and said, "You really want this apple?"

"You heard me," Tamerlane said in a flat voice. "That apple belongs to me."

Peter looked at the boy who was preparing to hit him and remembered the birthday party three weeks before when Barry had been so warm, so friendly. Now he was scrunching up his face to make himself look as mean as possible. What gave him the idea that when he was at school he could do anything or take anything he wanted?

Peter dared take his eyes off Barry for a moment and saw the circle of excited, fearful faces pressing in. Eyes were wide, mouths hung open. Someone was about to be floored by the terrible Tamerlane and there was nothing anyone could do about it. What made pink, plump Barry so powerful? Immediately, from out of nowhere, Peter had the answer. "It's obvious," he thought. "We do. We've dreamed him up as the school bully. He's no stronger than any of us. We've dreamed up his power and his strength. We've made him into what he is. When he goes home, no one believes in him as a bully and he just becomes himself."

Barry spoke again. "S'your last chance. Gimme the apple or I'll knock you into the middle of next week."

In reply Peter raised the apple to his mouth and took an enormous bite. "You know what," he said slowly through his mouthful. "I don't believe you. In fact, I'll tell you something for nothing. I don't even believe you exist."

There was a gasp from the crowd, and a few giggles too. Peter sounded so sure of himself. Perhaps it was true.

Even Barry frowned and stopped swaying. "What was that?"

All Peter's fear had gone. He stood right in front of Barry, smiling as though he rather pitied him for not existing. After weeks of wondering whether life was really a dream, Peter had decided that Tamerlane the bully certainly was one, and that if he hit Peter in the face with all his strength, it would hurt him no more than a shadow could.

Barry had recovered and was getting ready for the kill.

Peter took another bite of the apple. He put his face close up to Barry's and peered at him as though he were nothing more than a funny picture on a wall. "You're just a fat little pink jelly . . . with metal teeth."

There was a hoot of laughter in the crowd that spread and took hold. There were cackles and giggles and whoops. Children clutched at each other or slapped their knees. They were acting up, of course. They wanted to show each other they were no longer afraid. Fragments of the insult were tossed around the crowd. "Pink jelly . . . Metal teeth . . . A jelly with teeth!" Peter knew his remark was cruel. But what did it matter? Barry wasn't real anyway. He was flushing bright pink, brighter than any jelly. He was hating this.

Peter pressed on before Barry could find his anger. "I've been to your house. Remember? On your birthday. You're just a nice, ordinary little boy. I saw you helping your mommy with the washing up . . ."

"Aaaaaaah," sang the crowd in a long descending note of mock affection.

"It's not true," Barry spat out. His eyes were bright.

"And I looked in your bedroom and saw your teddy tucked up in your bed."

"AAAAAAAH!" cried the crowd.

The sound tumbled from an even higher note, swooping down in scorn. "Oooooooh, lickle ickle Basy . . . Teddy weddy . . . Aaaah."

Of course there was not one single child there who did not still secretly love a battered old stuffed animal and cuddle it at night. But how wonderful to know that the bully had one too.

Barry Tamerlane probably still had it in mind to whack Peter in the face. As the shouts and jeers rose, he raised his arm and weakly clenched his fist. And just then something terrible happened. He burst into tears. There was no disguising it. The tears came in quick trickles down both sides of his nose, and his breathing was no longer his own to control. His whole body heaved as he fought for little hard lumps of air. But the crowd knew no mercy.

"Lickle Basums wants his mama . . ."

"Wants his teddy weddy . . ."

"Ooooooh. Look at him . . ."

And now the crying came on so strong that poor Barry did not even have the strength to walk away. He simply stood in the circle of children and wept snottily into his hands. Everything and everyone was against him. No one believed in him. The dream bubble had burst and the bully had vanished with it.

Slowly the taunts and laughter subsided and an embarrassed silence settled on the crowd. The children began to drift away, back to their games. A teacher came hurrying across the playground, put her arms around the shoulders of the solitary boy, and led him away saying, "Poor little thing. Has someone been picking on you?"

For the rest of that morning in class Barry was subdued. He hunched over his work and would not look up or meet anyone's eye. He seemed to be trying to make himself look smaller or disappear altogether.

Peter, on the other hand, was feeling full of himself. He came in from the playground and took his place at his desk, right behind Barry, pretending to ignore the winks and grateful smiles all around him. He had thrashed the bully without lifting a finger, and nearly the whole school had seen it. He was a hero, a conqueror, a superman. There was nothing he could not achieve with his brilliant, cunning intelligence.

But as the morning passed, he began to feel rather different. His words began to haunt him. Had he really said them? He became aware of the crumpled figure of Barry Tamerlane in front of him. Peter leaned forward and tapped him on the back with a ruler. But Barry shook his head and would not turn. Peter winced as he remembered more of what he had said. He tried to remind himself of how awful Barry had been. Peter tried to concentrate on his victory, but he no longer felt good about it. He had mocked Barry for being fat and having braces and a teddy and for helping his mom. He had wanted to defend himself and teach Barry a lesson, but he had ended up making him an object of scorn and contempt for the whole school. His words had hurt far more than a straight punch to the nose. He had crushed Barry. Who was the bully now?

On his way out to lunch Peter dropped a note on Barry's desk. It read: "Do you want to play soccer? P.S. I've got a teddy, too, and I have to help with the dishes. Peter."

Barry had been dreading facing everyone at the next playtime, so he gladly accepted. The two boys got up a game and made a point of being on the same team. They helped each other score goals and walked off at the end arm in arm. It didn't make sense for anyone to go on jeering at Barry. He and Peter became friends, not close friends exactly, but friends all the same. Barry pinned Peter's note to the wall above his desk in his bedroom, and the bully, like all bad dreams, was soon forgotten.

CHAPTER SIX

THE BURGLAR

ALL THE NEIGHBORS were talking about the burglar. Months ago he had broken into a house at the bottom of the street. He had wriggled in through a back window in the full light of a sunny midafternoon when the house was empty. He had made off with knives and forks and a painting. Now he was working his way up the street, a house on one side, then a house on the other.

"What a nerve!" people kept saying. "He's bound to get caught. Last night he did number eight, next week it will be number nine."

But no, he would wait for three weeks, or four, and he would leapfrog to number eleven. Then he would come the very next day and rob number twelve. He stole televisions, video machines, computers, statues, jewels. He knew how to pick locks, scale drainpipes, silence burglar alarms, slide back window catches, make friends with angry dogs, and stroll away with his loot in the middle of the day without being seen. He was a magician, a maestro of theft. He was invisible, silent, and weightless. He left no footprints in the garden beds or fingerprints on door handles.

The police were baffled. Two plainclothesmen were sent to watch over the

street in an unmarked car. Everyone
knew who they were. They sat doing
crosswords and eating sandwiches until
they were called away to more important
work. Half an hour later the burglar
struck again and carried off a box of
expensive perfumed soap and a silver-
topped walking stick from the home of
Mrs. Goodgame, a rich old lady with
yellow protruding teeth who lived alone.
The stick had belonged to her great-
grandfather, a famously fierce mission-
ary. He used it to beat African children
when they didn't study their Bible
lessons.

"It was of great sentimental value!"
Mrs. Goodgame wailed when she came to
tell the news to Peter's mother. "It traveled around the world three times in the
nineteenth century. And my soap, my
precious soap!"

"I'm glad he took that stinking stick,"
Peter said to Kate after Mrs. Goodgame

had left. "I hope that burglar breaks it over his knee."

Kate nodded fiercely. "I wish he had taken her teeth!" The fact was that Mrs. Goodgame, even though she had a name that made her sound fun, was not liked by the children in the street. She was one of those rare unhappy grown-ups who are profoundly irritated by the fact that children exist. When they played outside, she shouted at them from her front window for "gathering outside my house." She believed that all the litter that blew onto her lawn was put there by mischievous children. If a ball or a toy landed in her garden, she darted out and confiscated it. She was always in a bad mood, and things were made worse for her because the children teased her. Making her angry was something of a sport. Peter's parents said she was a little mad and deserved pity. They always tried to be pleasant to her. But for the children it was hard to feel pity for a grown-up with yellow fangs who was chasing you up the street.

So Peter did not mind so much when Mrs. Goodgame's soap and stick were carried away. He was beginning to feel some respect for this burglar. He decided to call him Soapy Sam. What a daredevil he was to take on a whole street, house after house, in ascending order. He seemed to be asking to be caught!

The months passed, a few more houses were done. Numbers fifteen, nineteen, twenty-two, twenty-seven. There could be no doubt about it. Soapy was heading Peter's way, number thirty-eight.

He had spent much time making calculations with pencil and paper. As far as he could tell, there was no pattern to the house numbers the burglar chose. But if he came at all, the burglar would be due in their house in less than two weeks. Perhaps it would be passed by. Peter knew he would be disappointed if that happened. Without telling anyone, he had decided that he was going to be the one who would catch Soapy Sam.

The weekend before Soapy was expected, Thomas and Viola Fortune made preparations. Thomas Fortune fastened shut the windows by drilling long screws through the frames. He installed stronger locks on the front and back doors, and he padlocked the gate around the side of the house. He tried to put in a do-it-yourself burglar alarm, but he hit his thumb with a hammer while tacking electric wire to a wall, which put him in a terrible mood. Worse still, the alarm didn't work. There was no time to get a proper one in place, and besides, it wouldn't stop Soapy Sam. Viola Fortune carried her favorite gardening tools indoors. She went from room to room gathering up paintings, ornaments, lamps, and valuable books and locked them in a cup-

board at the top of the house. Peter and
Kate hid their favorite toys under their
beds. It was as if what was coming up the
street was a hurricane, a whirlwind, a
typhoon that would snatch away everything they had. In fact, it was just one little old thief who was rather clever at his
job. But was he cleverer than Peter?

Peter began to plan his campaign. His
first problem was this: If he was going to
catch the thief, he was going to have to
be at home, and that meant getting off
from school. He could fake an illness, but
he had to be careful. He had to pitch it
exactly right. If he pretended too hard,
one of his parents would take time off
from work to look after him. Soapy Sam
would see there were people in the house
and move on up the street. On the other
hand, if Peter didn't appear ill enough,
he would be sent to school with a note
excusing him from gym. If he got it right,
he would be allowed to stay at home by

himself, with Mrs. Farrar, their kindly old neighbor, popping in every hour or so to check on him.

In the afternoons, home from school, he locked his bedroom door and practiced looking droopy. Wanting to make himself look pale, he dusted his face with flour. In the mirror he resembled a corpse come to life. He chewed peppercorns to raise his temperature. It worked too well. His mouth and throat seemed to catch fire, and his temperature soared so that he would have been rushed to the hospital. He wondered if a sprained ankle might suit him better. He limped up and down the tiny floor space of his bedroom. He looked more like a boy who was turning into a crab.

He was still perfecting his illness three days later when he heard the news from his mother. Mr. and Mrs. Baden–Baden at number thirty-four had been burgled. Only two months before, they had spent thousands on the very latest alarm system, with red and blue warning lights, sonic intruder devices, and a whooping siren. Soapy Sam seemed to have melted through the walls of their house and stolen a four-hundred-year-old tennis racket in a glass frame and a worm-eaten piano stool that Mozart was supposed to have sat on for two minutes at the age of five.

"Isn't that shocking?" Viola Fortune said.

"It's outrageous," Peter agreed.

But when his mother had gone, he punched the air in excitement. Soapy Sam was on his way! Peter had no reason to believe that his own house, number thirty-eight, would be next. He had made up his mind because he wanted it to happen, and somehow that seemed enough. Nor could he possibly know when the next break-in would be. But he had made a guess and decided that Soapy Sam

would be visiting in four or five days'
time.

Now, while Peter was making arrangements to be ill, he was also wondering
how he was going to trap the thief. He
daydreamed his way through trapdoors,
a net that fell from the ceiling, a gold
ingot covered in Super Glue, electric
cable wired to door handles, toy guns,
poisoned darts, lassos, pulleys and ropes,
hammers, springs, halogen lights and
fierce dogs, smokescreens, laser beams,
piano wire, and a rake. But Peter was not
a fool. He knew perfectly well that all
these ideas could work, but he also knew
that for a ten-year-old, making them
work was almost impossible.

That Saturday morning he lay on his
bed thinking. He found himself staring at
the old mousehole in the baseboard near
his bed. There were no mice in there
these days, and the hole seemed to go on
forever under the wall and down below

the floorboards. Then he stared up at the shelf where he kept his most valuable possessions and suddenly he saw the solution. Whatever he did, it had to be simple. There was the mousehole, and up there was last year's birthday present, appearing to look at him and say, "Use me! Use me!"

He sat at his table, took a sheet of paper, and with a trembling hand wrote a short letter, perhaps the most important letter he had ever written. Then he sealed it in an envelope that he wrote on and took downstairs to the desk where all the household bills were kept. He tucked it away, just out of sight but easily found. Written in block capitals on that envelope were the words "To be opened in the event of my sudden death."

Viola Fortune prided herself on her deep understanding of her children. She knew their moods, their weaknesses, their worries, and everything else about them far better than they knew themselves. For example, she knew when Peter and Kate were tired, long before they actually felt tired. She knew when they were really in a bad mood, even if they thought they were in a good one. That Sunday evening she quietly observed that Peter was rather slow in coming to the supper table when called, that he finished his food, but with an effort that he could conceal from anyone except her, and that when he was offered seconds, his upper lip quivered in disguised disgust. And this was steak and crinkle-cut french fries under half a bottle of ketchup.

"Peter, darling. You don't look well," she said at last.

"I feel great," he said, and sighed and ran his hand across his face.

"I think you might need an early

night," Viola said.

"I don't think so," Peter said, but his mother noted wisely that he didn't say it with the usual force. When he was ordered into his pajamas after supper, he put up only token resistance. When she peeped into his bedroom twenty minutes later, he was already asleep. "He couldn't fool me," she thought as she tiptoed away. "He really isn't well."

Peter lay awake until midnight making his plans. In the morning his mother could see for herself how pale and droopy he looked. She took his temperature. Nothing too serious, but it was clear he could not go to school, however much he pleaded. He was well enough to read and watch TV, so arrangements were made with Mrs. Farrar. Peter was set up on the living room sofa.

"No bad thing if the house looks occupied," his father said when he came in to say good-bye. "Turn the TV volume right up. You'll keep the burglar out at least."

Everybody left. Peter turned off the TV and stretched out under the blanket listening to the creaks and murmurs of a house settling into silence. He did not expect a break-in just yet, not at half past nine in the morning. He was sure Soapy Sam did not get out of bed early. He slept until midday and ate a long, slow breakfast, planning his next move over cups of strong coffee and reading the papers for news of the arrest of old friends.

Sure enough, the morning was uneventful. Mrs. Farrar came by with some homemade cookies. Peter watched TV, read books, checked his equipment, and went about the house turning out one or two lights and drawing the living room curtains so that he could not be seen from the outside. From the street the house looked empty. He was beginning to feel restless. He ate the lunch that had been left for him, even though he was not hungry. He was bored with television and books, and most of all he was bored with waiting. He prowled through the rooms. He crept up to the windows and peeped out. The street was quiet, dull, thiefless. Perhaps this was all a stupid mistake. Perhaps he should be at school with his friends.

Taking care to bring his antiburglar equipment with him, he went upstairs to his room. By leaning out of the window he had a good view of the street in both directions. No one, nothing, not even a single passing car. He lay down on his bed and groaned. Catching burglars was supposed to be exciting, but this was the dullest, emptiest day he had ever spent. Pretending to be ill and doing nothing all morning had made him feel weary. He closed his eyes and drifted away.

It was not a sleep exactly, more of a

light doze. He was aware of himself on the bed, and he could hear sounds from outside through the open window. Footsteps first, approaching from a long way off and coming closer. Then a scraping, dragging sound, sharp and dry, like metal being dragged over stone, and that too grew louder and louder, then stopped. Peter was awake enough to know that he really ought to try and open his eyes. He ought to get off the bed and close the window. But he was comfortable where he was, his body was heavy and soft, like a balloon filled with water. It was an effort to move his eyelids. Now there was another disturbance outside, just below his window, a soft rhythmic padding, like footsteps but slower, as though someone were coming up a ladder. And the sound of difficult, bad-tempered breathing that grew louder by the second.

Peter came to his senses and opened his eyes. The open window filled his

vision. He could see the end of an aluminum ladder propped against the windowsill, and a hand, an old wrinkled hand, followed by another, groping over the ledge. Peter shrank back into the pillows. He was too terrified to remember his carefully thought-out plans. All he could do was watch. A head and shoulders appeared in the window frame. The face was obscured by a checked scarf and a tight black cap. The figure held still for a moment, staring into the room without seeing Peter. Then it began to climb through the window with irritable grunts and murmurs of "Blasted stupid thing!" until it was in and surveying the room, still without noticing Peter, who lay so still he must have looked like part of the pattern on the bedspread.

The burglar reached into a pocket, took out a pair of black gloves, and pulled them on quickly. Then he unwound the scarf and pushed the cap clear of his face.

But it wasn't a he at all. Peter couldn't help himself. He let out a cry of astonishment. The burglar looked straight at him without surprise.

"Mrs. Goodgame!" Peter whispered.

She smiled her yellow smile at him and arched her eyebrows. "Yes. I saw you there just as I was climbing in. I wondered when you were going to recognize me."

"But you were burgled last week. . . ."

She gave him a look, pitying his stupidity.

"You made it up so no one would suspect it's you . . . ?"

She nodded cheerily. She seemed much happier as a burglar. "Now, are you going to let me get on with my work and keep your mouth shut afterward, or am I going to have to kill you?"

Even as she was asking this important question, she was advancing into the room, looking around. "Not much here, really. But I will have that."

She plucked from a shelf a scale model of the Eiffel Tower that Peter had bought in Paris once on a school trip. She slipped it into her pocket.

It was at this moment that Peter remembered his plan. He picked up his camera from the bedside table. "Mrs. Goodgame?" he said mildly. As she turned from her study of Peter's toys, the flash went off in her face. And then again, flash . . . flash. Immediately after the third, Peter began rewinding the film.

"Hey, give me that camera, boy. Right away." Her voice rose to a shriek on these last two words. She stretched out a hand that shook with anger.

Peter slipped the film free. As he handed the camera to her, he leaned over the edge of the bed and rolled the canister of exposed film into the mousehole.

"Boy, what are you doing there? This camera is empty!"

"That's right," Peter said. "The pictures of you are right down there. You'll never get them out."

With a creak of knee joints, Mrs. Goodgame crouched down and looked. Then with short, ill-tempered gasps she got to her feet. "Oh, dear," she said, absentmindedly. "You're right. It looks like I will have to kill you after all." And with these words she pulled out a gun and pointed it at Peter's head.

He pressed himself back against the wall. "I'd rather you didn't," he said. "But if you insist, there's something you ought to know first. It's only fair I tell you."

Mrs. Goodgame gave a yellow, humorless smile. "Make it quick then."

Peter spoke quickly. "Somewhere in this house in an envelope marked 'To be opened in the event of my sudden death.' Inside it says that in this mousehole are pictures of a burglar and a murderer. They'll need a crowbar and a sledgehammer, but I'm sure they'll take the trouble."

It took at least a minute for all this information to be digested by Mrs. Goodgame, and all the while she kept the gun leveled at Peter's head. Finally she lowered the gun, but she did not put it away.

"Very clever," she snapped. "But you haven't worked it out very well at all. If I shoot you, the photos will be discovered and I'll be caught. But if I don't shoot you, you'll hand the pictures over to the police and I'll still be caught. So I might just as well shoot you for the fun of it. And as a punishment for making my life so difficult."

She released the catch on the gun with a loud click and raised it once more toward Peter. He was scrambling off the bed while trying to hold his hands above his head. It was not easy. He really did not want to be shot. His birthday was only weeks away and he was hoping for a new bike.

"But, Mrs. Goodgame," he stuttered. "I've thought about all that. If you'll promise to stop thieving and to return all the things you've taken, I'll try and fish the photos out and give them to you. Honest I will."

Her eyes narrowed as she considered. "Hmm. Getting all this stuff back won't be easy, you know."

"You could go around in the middle of the night and leave it on people's doorsteps."

Mrs. Goodgame put her gun away. Peter lowered his arms.

"You know," she said in a wheedling voice, "I was hoping to get all the way to the end of the street. Couldn't I just—"

"Sorry," Peter said. "It's got to stop now. That's my offer. If you don't like it, then go ahead and shoot me."

She turned and seemed to hesitate, and

for one anxious moment Peter thought she would do just that. But she took out her scarf and wound it over her mouth and pulled her cap down tight. She crossed to the window and began to climb out.

"You know, I've had an awful lot of fun these past few months. Now I'll have to go back to shouting at children."

"Yes," Peter said kindly. "You can't get arrested for that."

She flashed him one last yellow smile, and then she was gone. Peter heard the creak of her tread on the rungs and the scrape of the ladder being pulled away from the wall. He sat down on the edge of his bed and put his head in his hands and sighed. That was very, very close.

He was still sitting in this position when he heard footsteps thundering up the stairs. The door flew open and his father rushed in and crouched at Peter's side and took his hand.

"Thank God you're all right," Thomas Fortune said breathlessly.

"Yes," Peter said. "It was very, very—"

"You've been up here asleep," his father said. "That's just as well. You didn't hear a thing. He took the TV, and the blanket and all the soap from the bathroom. Cut a hole in the glass of a side window and undid the screws . . ."

While his father went on talking, Peter was staring at the mousehole. During the weeks that followed, he was to spend many hours on his stomach, searching in that hole with a length of straightened-out wire coat hanger. Whenever he passed Mrs. Goodgame in the street, she pretended not to know him. She never kept her word and returned the stolen goods, and meanwhile the burglaries continued right to the end of the street. She would go to jail if he could just find those photographs, so he kept on jiggling and poking with his piece of wire. But he never found that roll of film, nor did he ever find his model of the Eiffel Tower.

CHAPTER SEVEN

THE BABY

ONE AFTERNOON in spring, when the kitchen was filled with sunlight, Peter and Kate were told that their aunt Laura and her baby, Kenneth, would be coming to live with them for a while. No reason was given, but it was clear from their parents' solemn looks that all was not well with their aunt.

"Laura and the baby will take your room, Kate," their mother said. "You'll have to move in with Peter."

Kate nodded bravely.

"Is that all right with you, Peter?" his father asked.

Peter shrugged. There didn't seem to be much choice.

And so it was arranged. In fact, Peter looked forward to Laura's arrival. She was the youngest of his mother's many sisters and brothers, and he liked her. She was dangerous and fun. He had once watched her at a country fair leap off the top of a two-hundred-foot crane attached to an elastic rope. She had come hurtling out of the sky, and just before she was dashed to pieces on the grass, she had gone shooting up into the air again with a long scream of terror and hilarity.

Kate moved into Peter's room, bringing her newest game, a box of magic, with a wand and a book of spells. She also brought along a small detachment of thirty dolls. The same day a mountain of baby gear appeared in the house: a crib, a high chair, a playpen, a baby carriage, a stroller, an indoor swing, and five large bags of clothes and toys. Peter was suspicious. Surely one small person shouldn't need this much stuff. Kate, on the other hand, was crazy with excitement. Even on Christmas Eve she had never been this far gone.

The children were allowed to stay up late to greet the visitors. The sleeping baby was carried to the sofa and settled there. Kate knelt by it, as if she were in church, gazing into the infant face and occasionally sighing. Laura sat on the other side of the room and lit a cigarette with trembling hands. Peter could tell at a glance she was in no mood for fun or danger, unless, of course, you counted smoking. She replied to their mother's gentle remarks and questions with short answers and turned her head sharply at right angles to blow her smoke into a corner where no one sat.

Over the next few days they saw very little of Laura and rather a lot of baby Kenneth. Peter marveled at how one small person could take up so much space. In the hallway were the baby carriage and stroller; into the living room were crammed the playpen, the swing, and a great scattering of toys; and in the kitchen the high chair blocked the way to the cupboard where the cookies were kept.

And Kenneth himself was everywhere. He was one of those babies who are so good at crawling, they gain nothing by trying to walk. He lumbered across the carpet at alarming speed, like a military tank. He was a baby in the bloated style, with a great square jaw supporting a fat damp face of furious pink, with bright, determined eyes and nostril wings that flared like a sumo wrestler's whenever he did not immediately get what he wanted.

Kenneth was a grabber. If he saw an object within his reach that he could lift, his hot, wet fist would close around it and transfer it to his mouth. It was an appalling habit. He tried to eat the pilot who belonged in the cockpit of the model airplane Peter was gluing together. Kenneth also bit the wings. He ate Peter's homework. He chewed the pencils, the ruler, and the books. He crawled into the bedroom and tried to munch the camera Peter had been given for his birthday.

"He's crazy!" Peter yelled as he wiped his camera dry and his mother carried Kenneth away. "If he could get us in his mouth, he'd eat us all."

"It's only a phase," Kate said wisely. "We all used to do it." This calm, know-everything tone she had adopted since

Kenneth's arrival was also getting on Peter's nerves. She had copied it from their mother. Surely no one could deny that this baby was awful. Mealtimes were the worst. Kenneth had a way of turning food into muck. He mashed and squelched it until it dripped like glue, and smeared it over his arms, face, clothes, and high chair. The sight turned Peter's stomach. He had to eat with his eyes closed. And conversation was almost impossible because the baby yelled at the top of his lungs at almost every spoonful.

The baby had taken over the house. There was not a corner into which his yells, smells, and mad hyena laughter and grabbing little hands did not reach. He emptied cupboards and bookcases, tore up newspapers, knocked down lamps and full cartons of milk. No one seemed to mind. In fact, everyone—Peter's mother, his aunt, his sister, and his father—cooed with delight at every fresh outrage.

Things came to a head one late afternoon after school. It was midsummer, but it was raining and cold. Kate lay on her bed reading. Peter was kneeling on the floor. A marble craze was sweeping through the school, and he was a keen player. The day before, he had won from another boy the finest marble he had ever seen, a Green Gem. It was smaller than most and seemed to shine with its own light. He was using it now, rolling it across the carpet toward the large marmalade marble he always used for target practice. Just as the Green Gem left his hand, Kenneth's fat bald head appeared around the door. The marble rolled straight toward him, and he barged forward eagerly.

"Kenneth, no!" Peter shouted. But too late. The baby scooped up the marble and put it in his mouth. Peter started to scramble across the floor, intending to prize Kenneth's jaws apart. Then he stopped. It was horribly clear what had happened. The baby sat perfectly still. For a second his eyes bulged and a look of puzzled irritation passed across his face. Then he blinked, blinked again, and looked at Peter and smiled.

"No," Peter whispered. "He's swallowed it."

"Swallowed what?" Kate said, without looking up from her book of spells.

"My Green Gem, the marble I won yesterday."

Kate put on her calm, know-it-all voice. "Oh, that. I wouldn't worry. It's very small and smooth. It won't do him any harm."

Peter glared at Kenneth, who sat contentedly staring at his own hand. "I don't care about him. What about my marble?"

"It'll be fine," Kate said. "It'll come out the other end."

Peter shuddered. "Thanks a lot."

Kate closed her book of spells. She leaned down and tickled Kenneth. He laughed and crawled toward her bed. She pulled him up and sat him beside her on the bed. "Do you know what I think?" She said.

Peter said nothing. He knew he would be told.

"I think you're jealous of Kenneth."

How irritating his sister could be. "That's so stupid!" Peter said. "That's the stupidest thing I've ever heard. How could I be jealous of that thing?" He glared at the baby, who stared back with simple interest, his huge head wobbling.

"He's not a thing," Kate said. "He's a person. Anyway, it's simple. He's getting all the attention now instead of you."

Peter looked at her suspiciously. "You didn't make this up yourself. Who said it?"

His sister shrugged. "It's true anyway.

You aren't the youngest boy in the house anymore. That's why you're so horrid to him.'"

"Me horrid to him? He's the one who ate my marble. He's a lunatic. He's a nuisance. He's a monster!"

Kate's face was flushed with anger. She stood up and lifted Kenneth to the floor. "He's a dear little thing. And you are awful. It's time someone taught you a lesson." She snatched up her books and left the room in a hurry. The baby lumbered after her.

Half an hour later Peter wandered downstairs. Kate was slumped in an armchair in the living room with a book open on her lap. Kenneth was on the floor, peaceful for the moment as he chewed his way through an old magazine.

Peter took a chair on the far side of the room. He wanted to continue the argument. He wanted to know where Kate had gotten her ridiculous ideas from. But he wasn't sure how to begin. His sister was frowning at her book and fiddling with the black magic wand that came with it. Kenneth had noticed Peter at last and crawled toward him. Using Peter's leg as a support, the baby hauled himself upright until he stood unsteadily between the older boy's knees.

Peter stared over the baby's head at his sister. She did not look up. She was still angry with him. It was just as well the magic set was nothing more than a toy. He looked down at Kenneth again. The baby was staring deep into his eyes and frowning, as if searching for something in his mind, a memory, a lost clue to another life.

"Gaaaaa," Kenneth said quietly.

"Gaaaaa," Kate repeated from the other side of the room. She was pointing the wand at Peter.

"Gaaaaa gaaaaa," Kenneth repeated.

"Gaaaaa gaaaaa," Kate echoed and drew

a circle in the air. The room began to brighten and turn floor-over-ceiling and grow larger and larger, until it was the size of an enormous hall in a palace.

Peter was on his feet, swaying as he struggled to keep his balance. He clutched at a pillar. But it was alive and warm. It was a leg, a gigantic leg. Peter lifted his heavy wobbly head and tried to direct his unreliable gaze at the owner of the leg. He glimpsed a face, but it slipped from his view. He moved his huge head back and saw it again, a giant version of himself in school clothes, staring down at him with unconcealed disgust. Numbly Peter looked down at his own clothes—a ridiculous jumpsuit patterned with teddy bears and stained down the front with orange juice and chocolate. Terrible, terrible! He had swapped bodies with Kenneth.

In his surprise Peter let go of the leg

and fell back on the floor into a sitting position.

"Oops!" he heard a musical voice say for him.

This was awful, this was unfair, this was frightening. He was on the edge of tears, but he could not remember what it was that had upset him. His attention half drifted, half swam from one thing to another.

"Help me, someone!" he shouted. "Someone do something!" But what came from his lips was a succession of clumsy *shhh* sounds. His tongue wouldn't go where he told it, and he seemed to have only one tooth.

Tears were pouring down his face, and he was just drawing breath to fill his lungs and bawl out his sorrow when something powerful clamped under his armpits and he shot fifty feet into the air. His mouth hung open, he was dribbling in his amazement. He was staring into his aunt Laura's face, which was as sheer and colossal as a cliff. She looked like one of those American presidents carved out of a mountain.

Her voice, as rich and musical as a symphony orchestra, thundered about his head. "Five o'clock. Teatime, bathtime, and bed!"

"Put me down, Aunt Laura. It's me, Peter."

But what came out was "Aaa, agooo amama."

"That's right," she said encouragingly. "Tea, bath, and bed. Did you hear him?" she said to someone far away. "He's trying to talk."

Peter began to kick and struggle. "Put me down!" But now he was flying across the room at terrifying speed. Surely he would be smashed to pieces on the door frame. "Eeeek!" he squealed. Just in time they changed direction, and he was whisked through the kitchen and tipped into the high chair.

Afternoon sunlight pouring through the trees made shifting patterns on the wall of such beauty that Peter forgot all else.

He pointed and shouted. "Aark!"

Aunt Laura was humming softly to herself as she tied a bib around his neck. Well, at least he was in no danger of falling to the ground now. He would be able to inform her that he was the victim of a cruel magic trick. So he said in his most reasonable voice, "Ing ing eeen," and he would have said much more if his mouth had not been suddenly stoppered by a spoonful of boiled egg. The taste and smell, the color and texture and squelching sound overwhelmed his senses and scattered his thoughts. Egginess exploded in his mouth, a white and yellow fountain of sensation shot upward through his brain. His whole body lurched as he tried to point at the bowl Laura held. He *had* to have more.

"Aark," he shouted through his mouthful, spraying his arm. "Aark, aark, aark!"

"Yes," his aunt said soothingly. "You like egg."

Until the egg was finished, Peter could think of nothing else. When it was done, and before he could remember what he meant to be talking about, a beaker of orange juice distracted him with its itchy, tangy, noisy taste. Then mashed banana started arriving in his mouth. This food was so good he was *proud* to wear it in his hair and on his hands and face and chest.

Finally he reeled against the side of the chair. He was so full he could hardly blink. But he knew he had to speak out. He took it slowly this time, using the tip of his tongue to press against his single tooth.

"Aunt Laura," he said patiently. "I'm

not actually your baby. I'm Peter, and it was Kate who—"

"Yes," Laura agreed. "Agoo agoo is quite right. Look at the state of you. Head to toe in egg and banana. Bathtime!"

Now Peter was in Aunt Laura's arms and flying up the stairs. On the landing they flashed by Kate.

"Waaah!" he shouted at her. "Waaah waaah!"

"Cooeee!" she called back, holding up the magic wand.

Minutes later he was sitting in a bath the size of a small swimming pool, wavelets of warm water lapping around his chest. He knew he should be talking to his aunt, but for a moment he was more interested in smacking the surface of the water with his open palms. How intricate and unique each splash was, with droplets separating out as they rose in the air and tumbling back to make patterns and ripples. It was so wonderful, so hilarious.

"Wow, look at this," he found himself shouting. "Eee ink aark!" He was so excited that his arms and legs shot out straight and he tumbled backward. Aunt Laura caught him gently with a cupped palm behind his head.

Shocked to his senses, Peter remembered that he had to let her know who he was. "Awaba—" he started to say, but suddenly he shot upward out the water, like a missile from a submarine, and landed in a white towel as large as the back garden.

He was dried, powdered, diapered, buttoned into pajamas, carried into the bedroom, and set down in Kenneth's crib. Aunt Laura sang him a lilting, interesting song about a black sheep who was holding back on certain bags of wool for people he knew.

"Encore!" he shouted. "Unga!"

So she sang it again. Then she kissed him, raised the side of the crib, and quietly left the room.

Peter would have panicked if the song had not made him so happy and sleepy. Early-evening sunlight played against the drawn curtains, which stirred mysteriously. Birds trilled their impossible songs. He listened intently. What was he going to do? What if Laura went back home and took him with her? He tried to sit up and think, but he was too tired to lift his huge head from the mattress.

He heard the door open and footsteps crossing the room. Kate's face appeared between the bars. She was smirking.

"Kate," he hissed. "Get me out of here. Go and get the wand."

She shook her head. "Serves you right."

"I've got to do my homework," Peter pleaded.

"Kenneth's doing it for you."

"He'll mess it up. Please, Kate. I'll give

you all my marbles. Anything you want."
She smiled. "You're much nicer like this."

She put her hands through the bars and
tickled his belly. He tried not to laugh,
but it was hopeless.

"Night night, fat baby," she whispered,
and then she was gone.

The following morning, groggy from a
sleep that seemed to have lasted six
months, Peter was carried down to the
kitchen. Blearily he looked down at his
family from the high chair.

They waved and sang out cheerily,
"Morning, Kenneth."

"Wark," he croaked back. "Wark ork.
I'm not Kenneth. I'm Peter."

Everyone seemed happy with his reply.
It was then that he became aware of the
boy at the far end of the table, Kenneth
in Peter's body and Peter's school clothes.
He was staring at Peter with a look of
such loathing and disgust that it made
dark ripples in the air.

The boy looked away. He pushed his plate aside, stood up, and left the room. Peter felt a cold jolt of rejection. Immediately he began to cry.

"Oh, wassa matter den?" various people in the room began to say.

"He doesn't like me," Peter tried to tell them through his wails, "and it makes me feel terrible. Aaa waba lama waa!"

His tears were wiped away, Kenneth and Kate left for school, his parents dashed off to work, and half an hour later, newly dressed for the day in fresh pajamas, Peter found himself sitting on the living room floor, imprisoned in the playpen while Laura was busy upstairs.

Now at last he could plan his escape. Somewhere in the house was Kate's magic wand. If only he could wave it over his head . . .

With his fat weak hands gripping the bars of the playpen, he managed to pull himself upright. The bars rose another few inches above his head. There were no footholds, and he was not strong enough to climb over. He sat down. He would have to be lifted out. He would have to bring Laura down.

He was just about to shout out to her when his attention was caught by a bright yellow brick near his foot. Yellow, yellow, yellow, it sang out. It vibrated, it glowed, it hummed. He had to have it. He lunged forward, and his hand closed around it, but he could not really *feel* it, not enough anyway. He raised it to his mouth, and with his sensitive lips and gums and tooth he explored the woody, painty, yellowy, cubey taste of it, until he understood it all.

Then he saw a red plastic hammer, so red he could feel the heat of its color on his face. With his mouth and tongue and saliva he traveled around its ridges and angles and folds.

This was how Aunt Laura found him

ten minutes later, contentedly chewing the foot of a toy kangaroo.

The day passed in a blur of entertainments, meals, and an afternoon nap. Occasionally Peter would remember that he ought to be looking for the wand, and then his thoughts would be trapped by the brilliant taste of food so good he wanted to sink his whole body into it; or he would be tickled by songs with strange ideas that needed all his attention—a woman living in a shoe, a cow leaping over the moon, a cat in a well; or he would see one more thing he needed to get his mouth around.

In the late afternoon Aunt Laura brought him downstairs from his afternoon nap and put him down on the floor, outside the playpen this time. Refreshed by sleep, Peter decided to make a new start. The wand was probably in the kitchen. He was crawling toward the door when he noticed to his left a pair of feet in familiar shoes, *his* shoes. His gaze traveled up the legs to the face of the boy in the armchair. He was scowling.

This time Peter held down his fear. He knew there was only one way of dealing with this. He crawled to the legs, pulled himself into a standing position, and, still panting from the effort, addressed himself directly to Kenneth.

"Listen here. You've got to stop looking at me like that. You've got no reason to dislike me. There's nothing wrong with me. I'm all right really . . ."

Even as he was speaking these words, the room began to glow and turn and shrink. Suddenly Peter found himself sitting in the chair, with baby Kenneth standing between his knees, trying to tell him something.

Peter picked the baby up and put him on his lap. Cautiously Kenneth reached out his hand and pushed the tip of Peter's nose.

"Parp!" Peter said loudly.

The baby's hand shot back, the face briefly showed alarm, which dissolved into smiles and then laughter. If Peter had told the cleverest, funniest, stupidest joke in the universe, it could not have made anyone laugh more than Kenneth did now.

Peter looked over the baby's head at Kate sitting on the other side of the room. "I don't really think he's a monster. Actually, you know, I quite like him."

Kate said nothing. She did not believe him.

"I mean," Peter went on, "I think he's brilliant."

"Hmm," Kate said. She put down the wand. "If you really meant that, you'd come with me and take him to the park in his stroller." It was a challenge she was certain he would not accept.

"Yeah!" Peter said, to his sister's astonishment. Still holding the baby, he got to his feet. "Let's go. There'll be some amazing things for him to look at."

Kate stood up too. "Peter, what's got into you?" But her brother did not hear her. As he carried Kenneth out into the hall, he was starting to sing at full volume, "Baa baa, black sheep, have you any wool . . ."

CHAPTER EIGHT

THE GROWN-UP

EVERY AUGUST the Fortune family rented a small fisherman's cottage on the Cornish coast. Anyone who saw the place would have to agree it was a kind of paradise. You stepped out of the front door into an orchard. Beyond it was a tiny stream—hardly more than a ditch but useful for damming up. Farther on, behind a thicket, ran a disused railway track that had once brought out ore from a local tin mine. Half a mile along was a boarded-up tunnel that the children were forbidden to enter. Around the back of the cottage were a few square yards of scrubby back garden that gave directly onto a broad horseshoe of bay fringed with fine yellow sand. At one end of the bay were caves just deep and dark enough to be scary. At low tide there were rock pools. In the parking lot behind the bay there was an ice cream truck from late morning till dusk. There were half a dozen cottages grouped along the bay, and the Fortunes knew and liked the other families who came in August. More than a dozen children aged two to fourteen made up a ragged group who played together and were known, at least to themselves, as the Beach Gang.

By far the best times were the evenings, when the sun sank into the

Atlantic and the families gathered in one of the back gardens for a barbecue. After they had eaten, the grown-ups would be far too content with their drinks and their endless stories to set about putting the children to bed, and this was when the Beach Gang would drift away into the smooth calm of dusk, back to all their favorite daytime places. Except now there was the mystery of darkness and strange shadows, and the cooling sand beneath their feet, and the delicious feeling as they ran about in their games that they were playing on borrowed time. It was way past bedtime, and the children knew that sooner or later the grown-ups would stir themselves out of conversations and the names would ring out in the night air—Charlie! Harriet! Toby! Kate! Peter!

Sometimes, when the shouts of the grown-ups could not reach the children at the far end of the beach, they sent

Gwendoline. She was the big sister of three of the children in the Beach Gang. Because there was not enough room at her family's cottage, Gwendoline was staying with the Fortunes. She had the bedroom next to Peter's. She seemed so sad, so wrapped up in her thoughts. She was a grown-up—some said she was as old as nineteen—and she sat with them all the time, but she didn't join in their chat. She was a medical student and she was getting ready for an important exam. Peter thought about her a lot, though he wasn't sure why. She had very green eyes and hair that was so ginger you could almost say it was orange. She sometimes stared at Peter long and hard, but she rarely spoke to him.

When she came to collect the children, she came ambling slowly across the beach, barefoot and in ragged shorts, and she only looked up when she reached them. She spoke in a quiet, sad, musical voice. "C'mon, you lot. Bed!" And then, without waiting to hear their protests or repeat herself, she would turn and walk away, scuffing the sand as she went. Was she sad because she was a grown-up and wasn't really enjoying it? It was hard to tell.

It was in the Cornish summer of his twelfth year that Peter began to notice how different the worlds of children and grown-ups were. You could not exactly say that the parents never had fun. They went for swims, but never for longer than twenty minutes. They liked a game of volleyball, but only for half an hour or so. Occasionally they could be talked into hide-and-seek or freeze tag or building a giant sand castle, but those were special occasions. The fact was that all grown-ups, given half the chance, chose to sink into one of three activities on the beach: sitting around talking, reading newspapers and books, or snoozing.

Their only exercise (if you could call it that) was long boring walks, and these were nothing more than excuses for talking. On the beach they often glanced at their watches and, long before anyone was hungry, started telling each other that it was time to start thinking about lunch or supper.

They invented errands for themselves—to the odd-job man who lived half a mile away, or to the garage in the village, or to the nearby town on shopping expeditions. They came back complaining about the holiday traffic, but *they* were the holiday traffic. These restless grown-ups made constant visits to the telephone booth at the end of the lane to call their relatives or their work or their grown-up children. Peter noticed that most grown-ups could not begin their day happily until they had driven off to find a newspaper, the right newspaper. Others could not get through the day without cigarettes. Others had to have beer. Others could not get by without coffee. Some could not read a newspaper without smoking a cigarette *and* drinking coffee. Adults were always snapping their fingers and groaning because someone had returned from town and forgotten something; there was always one more thing needed, and promises were made to get it tomorrow—another folding chair, shampoo, garlic, sunglasses, clothespins—as if the vacation could not be enjoyed, could not even begin, until all these useless items had been gathered up. Gwendoline, on the other hand, was different; she simply sat in a chair all day, reading a book.

Meanwhile Peter and his friends never knew the day of the week or the hour of the day. They surged up and down the beach, chasing, hiding, battling, invading, in games of pirates or aliens from space. In the sand they built dams, canals, fortresses, and a water zoo that they stocked with crabs and shrimps. Peter and the older children made up stories they said were true to terrify the little ones. Sea monsters with tentacles that crawled out of the surf and seized children by the ankles and dragged them into the deep. Or the madman with seaweed hair who lived in the cave and turned children into lobsters. Peter worked so hard on these stories that he found himself unwilling to go into the cave alone, and when he was swimming he shuddered when a strand of seaweed brushed against his foot.

Sometimes the Beach Gang wandered inland to the orchard, where they were building a camp. Or they ran along the old track to the forbidden tunnel. There was a gap in the boards and they dared each other to squeeze through into total darkness. Water dripped with a hollow, creepy, plopping echo. There were scurrying sounds that they thought might be rats, and there was always a dank sooty breeze that one of the big girls said was the breath of a witch. No one believed her, but no one dared walk more than a few paces in.

These summer days started early and ended late. Sometimes, as he was getting into bed, Peter would try to remember how the day had begun. The events of the morning seemed to have happened weeks before. There were times when he was still struggling to remember the beginning of the day when he fell asleep.

One evening after supper Peter got into an argument with one of the other boys whose name was Henry. The trouble started over a chocolate bar, but the argument soon developed into a bout of name-calling. For some reason all the other children, except of course Kate, sided with Henry. Peter threw the bar of chocolate down into the sand and walked off by himself. Kate went indoors to get a Band-Aid for a cut on her foot. The rest of the group wandered off along the shore. Peter turned and watched them go. He heard laughter. Perhaps they were talking about him. As the group moved farther away in the dusk, its individual members were lost to view and all that could be seen was a blob that moved and stretched this way and that. More likely they had forgotten all about him and were playing a new game. Peter continued to stand with his back to the sea. A sudden cool wind made him shiver. He looked toward the cottages. He could just make out the low murmur of adult conversation, the sound of a wine cork being pulled, the musical sound of a woman's laughter, perhaps his mother's. Standing there that August evening between the two groups, the sea lapping around his bare feet, Peter suddenly grasped something very obvious and terrible: one day he would leave the group that ran wild up and down the beach, and he would join the group that sat and talked. It was hard to believe, but he knew it was true. He would care about different things, about work, money and taxes, checkbooks, keys and coffee, and talking and sitting, endless sitting.

These thoughts were on his mind as he got into bed that night. And they were not exactly happy thoughts. How could he be happy at the prospect of a life spent sitting down and talking? Or doing errands and going to work. And never playing, never *really* having fun. One day he would be an entirely different person. It would happen so slowly he would not even notice, and when it had, his brilliant, playful eleven-year-old self would be as far away, as peculiar and as difficult to understand as all grown-ups seemed to him now. And with these sad thoughts he drifted into sleep.

The following morning Peter Fortune woke from troubled dreams to find himself transformed into a giant person, an adult. He tried to move his arms and legs, but they were heavy and the effort was too much for him so early in the day. So he lay still and listened to the birds outside his window and looked about him. His room was much the same, though it did seem a great deal smaller. His mouth was dry, he had a headache, and he was feeling a little dizzy. It hurt when he blinked. He had drunk too much wine the night before, he realized. And perhaps he had eaten too much as well, because his stomach felt tight. And he had been talking too much, because his throat was sore. He groaned and rolled over onto his back. He made a huge effort and managed to raise his arm and get his hand to his face so that he could rub his eyes. The skin along the line of his jaw rasped under his touch like sandpaper. He would have to get up and shave before he could do anything else. And he would have to make a move because there were things that needed doing, errands to run, jobs to do. But before he could stir, he was startled by the sight of his hand. It was covered in thick curly black hairs! He stared at this great fat thing with its sausage-sized fingers and began to laugh. Even the knuckles sprouted hairs. The more he looked at it, especially when he clenched it, the more it resembled a toilet brush.

He got himself upright and sat on the edge of the bed. He was naked. His body was hard, bony, and hairy all over, with new muscles in his arms and legs. When at last he stood up he almost cracked his head on one of the low beams of his attic room. "This is ridic-" he started to say, but his own voice astonished him. It sounded like a cross between a lawn mower and a foghorn. "I need to brush my teeth and gargle," he thought. As he crossed the room to the hand basin, the floorboards creaked under his weight. His knee joints felt thicker, stiffer. When he got to the basin, he had to cling to it while he examined his face in the mirror. With its mask of black stubble, it looked like an ape was staring back at him.

He found he knew just what to do when it came to shaving. He had watched his father often enough. When he finished, the face looked a little more like his own. In fact, rather better, less puffy than his eleven-year-old face, with a proud jaw and a bold stare. Rather handsome, he thought.

He dressed in the clothes that were lying on a chair and went downstairs. "Everyone's going to get a shock," he thought, "when they see I've grown ten years older and a foot taller in the night." But of the three adults slouched around the breakfast table, only Gwendoline glanced up at him with a flash of brilliant green eyes and quickly looked away. His parents simply muttered, "G'morning," and went on reading their papers. Peter still felt strange in his stomach. He poured his coffee and took up the paper that was folded by his plate and scanned the front page. A strike, a scandal about guns, and a meeting of the leaders of several important countries. He found he knew the names of all the presidents and ministers and he knew their stories and what they were after. His stomach still felt odd. He sipped the coffee. It tasted foul, as if burned cardboard had been mashed up and boiled in bathwater. He went on sipping anyway because he didn't want anyone to think that he was really eleven years old.

Peter finished his toast and stood up. Through the window he could see the Beach Gang running along the shoreline toward the cave. What a waste of energy so early in the day!

"I'm going to phone my work," Peter announced importantly to the room, "and I'm going to go for a stroll." Was there ever anything duller and more grown-up than a stroll? His father grunted. His mother said, "Fine," and Gwendoline stared at her plate.

In the hallway he dialed his assistant at the laboratory in London. All inventors have at least one assistant.

"How's the anti-gravity machine coming along?" Peter asked. "Did you get my latest drawings?"

"Your drawings made everything clear," the assistant said. "We made the changes you suggested, then we switched the machine on for five seconds. Everything in the room started floating about, just as you said. Before we try again, we're going to have to screw the tables and chairs to the floor."

"I don't want you to try again until I'm back from vacation," Peter said. "I want to see it for myself. I'll drive back on the weekend."

When he had finished on the phone, he stepped out into the orchard and stood by the stream. It was a beautiful day. The water flowing under the wooden footbridge made a lovely sound, and he was excited about his new invention. But for some reason he did not feel like moving away from the house. He heard a sound behind him and turned. Gwendoline was standing in the doorway, watching him. Peter felt the tightness in his stomach again. It was a cold, falling sensation. He felt weak in his knees. Gwendoline rested her arm on the rim of the ancient water barrel that stood by the front door. Morning sunlight, broken by the leaves of the apple trees, bobbed about her shoulders and in her hair. In all his twenty-one years Peter had never seen anything so, well, perfect, delicious, brilliant, beautiful . . . there was no word good enough for what he saw. Her green eyes were fixed on his.

"So you're going for a walk," she said lightly.

Peter could hardly trust himself to speak. He cleared his throat. "Yes. Want to come?"

They went down through the orchard to the raised cinder path where the railway track had once been. They talked about nothing in particular—about vacation, the weather, newspaper stories— anything to avoid talking about themselves. She put her smooth cool hand in his as they walked along. Peter seriously thought he might float off to the tops of the trees. He had heard about boys and girls, men and women, falling in love and feeling crazy, but he had always thought that people made too much of it. After all, how much can you really like someone? And in movies those bits which they always had to have, when the hero and heroine took time off to get soppy and gaze into each other's eyes and kiss had always seemed to him ridiculous time-wasting junk that did nothing more than hold up the story for several minutes on end. Now here he was, melting away at the mere touch of Gwendoline's hand, and he wanted to shout, to roar for joy.

They came to the tunnel, and without stopping to talk about it, they stepped through the gap in the boards, into the cold smoky blackness. They clung to each other as they went farther in, and giggled when they trod in puddles. The tunnel was not very long. Already they could see the far end, glowing like a pink star. Halfway along they stopped. They stood close. Their arms and faces were still warm from the sun's heat. They stood

close together and to the sound of scurrying animals and water plop-plopping
into puddles they kissed, and kissed
again. Peter knew that in all the years of
a happy childhood, and even in its very
best moments, like playing out with the
Beach Gang on a summer's evening, he
had never done anything better, anything
so thrilling and strange as kiss Gwendoline in the railway tunnel.

As they walked on toward the light,
she told him how one day she would be a
doctor and a scientist and she would
work on new cures for deadly diseases.
They stepped blinking into the sunshine
and found a place under the trees where
blue flowers grew on slender bendy
stems. They lay on their backs, eyes
closed, side by side in the long grass, sur-
rounded by murmuring insects. He told
her about his invention, the anti-gravity
machine. They could set off together

soon, climb into his green open-topped two-seater sports car and drive through the narrow lanes of Cornwall and Devon to London. They would stop at a restaurant along the way and order up chocolate mousse and ice cream and lemonade by the bucket. They would arrive at midnight outside the building. They would ride up in the elevator. He would unlock the laboratory and show her the machine, with its dials and warmly glowing lights. He would throw the switch, and together they would bump and tumble gently in the air with the tables and chairs. . . .

He must have fallen asleep in the grass as he was telling her this. "Sports car," he thought dozily, "chocolate mousse, stay up as late as I want, and Gwendoline . . . " It was at this point that he realized he was staring not at the sky but at his bedroom ceiling. He got out of bed and went to his window, which overlooked the beach. He could see the Gang, way in the distance. The tide was out, the rock pools were waiting. He slipped on his shorts and a T-shirt and hurried downstairs. It was late, everyone had finished breakfast long ago. He gulped down a glass of orange juice, took a bread roll and ran outside, across the tiny back garden and onto the beach. The sand was already hot under his feet, and his parents and their friends were already set up with their books and beach chairs and umbrellas.

His mother waved at him. "That was a good sleep. You needed that."

His friends had seen him and were calling, "Peter, Peter, come and look!"

Excited, he began to run toward them, and he must have been halfway when he stopped and turned to look at the grown-ups one more time. In the shade of the beach umbrellas they leaned in toward each other as they talked. He felt differently about them now. There were things they knew and liked that for him were only just appearing, like shapes in a mist. There were adventures ahead of him after all.

As usual, Gwendoline was sitting apart with her books and papers, studying for her exam. She saw him and raised her hand. Was she simply adjusting her sunglasses, or was it a wave? He would never know.

He turned and faced the ocean. It was sparkling, right to the wide horizon. It stretched before him, vast and unknown. One after the other the endless waves came tumbling and tinkling against the shore, and they seemed to Peter like all the ideas and fantasies he would have in his life.

He heard his name called again. His sister, Kate, was dancing and hopping on the wet sand. "We've found treasure, Peter!" Behind her, Harriet was standing on one leg, hands on hips, drawing a circle in the sand with her big toe. Toby

and Charlie and the little ones were jostling to take turns leaping off a rock into a salt-water puddle. And behind all this human movement the ocean bobbed and folded and slid, for nothing could keep still, not people, not water, not time.

"Treasure!" Kate called again.

"I'm coming," Peter shouted. "I'm coming!" and he began to sprint toward the water's edge. He felt nimble and weightless as he skimmed across the sand. "I'm about to take off," he thought. Was he daydreaming, or was he flying?